CW01661547

Once Upon a Christmas Tree

Lulu Moore

Cover Design by Sam Palencia at Ink and Laurel

Interior Design by Cleo Moran, Devoted Pages Designs

Editing by Perfectly Write Editing

To Christmas Miracles

Dear Readers,

Welcome to The Valentine Nook Chronicles, a brand-new series in the Luluverse. I'm so happy to have you here and introduce you to a whole host of new characters I know you're going to fall in love with.

One note I wanted to share, while Once Upon a Christmas Tree focuses on Alex and Haven, this prequel is as much an introduction to the entire Burlington family. As such ends with an HEA to be continued, because it wouldn't be fun if it was over too quickly.

But don't worry, there's still more spice than a pumpkin-spiced latte, all the signature boy banter you've come to love from my books, and stockings full of swoon.

Happy reading, and happy holidays,

Lulu Xo

Merry
Christmas

Alexander

1

"Such a shame. Would have been a beautiful wedding. I read in *Hello!* that it cost a million—"

"All those flowers—"

"Such a shame—"

"What did they say?"

"Nothing, just that there's been a change in destination, and passenger manifest—"

"No Caroline Montegue?"

"No Caroline Montegue—"

"And we're not going to the Maldives?"

"Aspen—"

"But I haven't packed for snow—"

"We can go shopping—"

Lando groans next to me and utters something indecipherable under his breath. If I were one of the twins, I'd leave them to carry on a little longer, just so they can really dig themselves into a hole of embarrassment. But I don't get off on causing mischief like my younger brothers do.

Plus, time is of the essence.

I'm about to alert these two overly chatty stewards to our presence when someone with much more skill and practice at pointed throat-clearing does exactly that. He's also excellent at suddenly appearing at your side, as silent as a ninja, given no one had heard him come in. But James Winters prides himself on discretion, which is exactly why he's been with our family for two decades.

"When you've finished gossiping, there are tasks to complete that require you to do more than stand around," he snaps, dropping two heavy duffle bags onto the floor.

The two air stewards spin around so quickly I'm almost impressed neither of them fall over. As predicted, their eyes widen in surprise, though they manage to recover themselves quickly enough that their mouths stay closed.

But then I realize they haven't noticed Lando or me, only James.

"Mr. Winters, we do apologize. We were just saying…"

This time, I clear my throat, because I really don't want to hear any more about their shopping plans or their disappointment the *Wedding of the Year*—as one of the newspapers dubbed it—was called off. And given my eldest brother is drunk to the point where he's bumping into me while standing, I need to get him settled.

This is the level of drunk usually seen on Miles.

It's comical how slowly their bodies move in sync. I can almost hear the prayers that they won't find Lando and me standing here. Too bad.

"Oh, Your Grace. Lord Burlington..." starts the one on the left, her eyes nearly falling out of her head. The one on the right composes herself much quicker.

James holds his hand up to silence her, allowing me the opportunity to speak instead. He already knows I'm not interested in hearing their profuse apologies, and I don't think he is either. It's certainly not the first time I've walked in on people talking about my family, it won't be the last.

"Are my brothers here? Has the plane been cleared?"

Their look of genuine confusion has me cursing the twins. *Again.*

One job. They had one bloody job, which was to get here before Lando and me, remove all the paraphernalia I know they've decorated the plane with, and restore it to its former beige glory so no one was any the wiser.

"No, my lord. We were only informed this minute there was a change of plans. We weren't expecting you quite so soon. But the pilots are on board running through their checks, so we'll be ready to leave imminently."

James's eyes dart from a swaying Lando and back to me, along with a slight purse of his lip. "Lord Alex, give me five minutes, we'll clear the plane and then get you settled. I'll find out the ETA of your brothers. I believe Lord Miles went back to fetch his snowboard."

I hold in the eye roll and check my watch. I thought two hours was plenty of time to get here and get organized. Pulling out my phone, I dial Hendricks, the more responsible one of the two, but only by a sliver on the very best of days if you catch him in the right light. Though it's possibly only the illusion of responsibility that has shone on him since he became a father.

Lando veers into me again. I hang up before it rings out, turning to James, who, I can tell, is seething.

As the Burlington family director of operations, he oversees the team managing the day to day of our lives. He joined us after serving two decades in the armed forces, and he's never lost the military precision with which he expects everything to run. It's highly probable our entire family would implode if he ever left, which is why he's earning the salary of a multinational CEO, because my mother's greatest fear is that one day James might decide he's had enough of our bullshit and quite sensibly leave.

After the last few months, I definitely couldn't blame him.

After the last twelve hours, I'd send him on his way myself with a massive severance, and a case of whiskey.

I clap a hand on his shoulder. "Don't worry, they'll be here soon. I'm going to go ahead and board, then we can be wheels up as soon as they arrive."

"Yes, my lord." His mouth rolls into a hard line. "I should point out I've not actually been in the plane yet…"

The way his sentence tails off tells me Hendricks and Miles were let loose in there.

Give me strength.

I turn to Lando, resisting the urge to lift his sunglasses and check he's still conscious. "Can you wait here with James?"

"No."

I sigh, because I should have known better than to ask. Pushing through the big swing doors to the hangar where our family plane is kept, Lando is hot on my heels. Stopping before I jog up the narrow stairs, my foot hovers over the first step and I try again. "Lan, seriously, just wait here, will you?"

"This day isn't going to get any worse by whatever's in that cabin," he snaps, marching past me.

He stops dead in the entrance, which is exactly what I was afraid of, and it takes me three giant strides until I'm standing beside him. I can't help it. The moment I lay eyes on the cabin, a laugh belts out of me. The twins have truly outdone themselves.

A huge banner with the words *Too Late Now* painted across it drapes along the length of the plane, above the sofa. Down the other side hangs one that reads *R.I.P. Lando*. Five huge cock-shaped balloons float above each table and—I squint—are held down with testicle weights.

Every window blind is covered with a blown-up photo of Lando and Caroline, though on closer inspection, they're not that flattering. Especially the one of Caroline almost face-first in the snow from a family ski trip we took a few years ago.

She refused to join us again after that.

"Jesus," I mutter, holding a small breath and side-eyeing Lando for his reaction—it's possible there's a smile almost curving the left side of his mouth, though it could just be a burp.

For the first time since this entire shit show of a day began, he pulls off his sunglasses.

"This was what we'd have been greeted with pre-honeymoon?" he croaks eventually, knocking a cock balloon out of the way, only for it to bounce back and narrowly miss hitting him in the face. A slow, steady hiss passes through his lips. "Caroline would have lost her shit."

"She would." I nod, snatching up a napkin with *glad you got the prenup* scribbled over it in Miles's distinct scratchy black writing before Lando sees it.

Not that it matters anymore. At least the wedding was called off before the vows.

Glancing around the cabin, I have a feeling if Caroline *had* seen this, she likely would have called for a divorce anyway. No doubt exactly what Hendricks and Miles had planned.

Lando removes his morning suit jacket and tosses it onto the chair opposite, his dress shoes are kicked off next and fly through the air, landing unceremoniously under one of the tables. Picking up a boob-shaped cushion I hadn't noticed, he lies back on the sofa, tucks it under his head, and replaces his sunglasses.

I'm currently debating whether to join him or start on the job I gave the twins to do, but

I have no idea how much longer they'll be, and I really don't want to be sitting among a plethora of phallic-shaped objects. Though I'd take these over Christmas decorations any day of the week.

Yanking off the R.I.P. banner, I toss it through the doors and go back for *Too Late Now*, but the sound of footsteps and a door clanging has me spinning around.

"Where've you two bloody been?" I grumble at Hendricks and Miles as they saunter into the hangar like they have all the time in the world. Certainly enough time to change out of the penguin suits Lando and I are still wearing. "You were supposed to be here before us."

Identical twins, rarely told apart by anyone outside of our immediate family, Hendricks and Miles are a law unto themselves. They work off their own time—as the present situation attests—and are seldom apart. It was only during the summer before last that they stopped living together, when Hendricks was finally granted full custody of his son, and promptly moved back into Burlington Hall, where we were all raised.

Miles's cottage—albeit still on the Burlington estate—wasn't deemed suitable enough to raise a child in.

Miles props up his snowboard. "You gave us thirty minutes' notice, and we went back to get some clothes for us all. Can't exactly go in morning suits, can we?"

I roll my eyes. "I told you James was getting our clothes. I was with Lando and working on getting us the fuck out of here as quickly as possible, and you two were supposed to clear the plane."

"But James didn't know where my snowboard was," Miles shoots back, and I realize his snowboard is all he's carrying. There's nothing to suggest he brought anything else.

"So where *are* all our clothes?"

Hendricks drops his head, though it doesn't disguise the amused curl of his lip.

"Yeah. About that—"

"You're bloody unbelievable."

"Hey! I got you a hoodie."

"Thanks."

"You're welcome." Miles grins. The grin that always gets him out of trouble, because no one—and I mean *no one*—can resist it. Even now, when I want to throttle him, I can feel the amusement rolling up my throat. "Where's Lan?"

I nod toward the cabin.

"How drunk is he?"

"Drunk enough that he thought the floating cocks were funny."

Hendricks barks a loud laugh. "You don't need to be drunk for that. Cocks are funny all the time."

I shake my head, but the main doors into the building swing open again before I can add anything else. James marches across the hangar, only halting his pace for a fraction of a second as he spies one of the cock balloons, and gives it a wide berth. The two stewards and three of his team follow, carrying the duffle bags of clothes, several shopping bags, and four sets of skis.

James might not be too happy with his staff, but we're leaving him and his team to clear up the chaos we're creating by escaping, so I'd say they've done an excellent job on two hours' notice, especially as it's not even lunchtime yet.

"My lords, we're ready to leave when you are. Flight path has been logged and cleared."

"Great stuff. Saving the bloody day again, James." Hendricks slaps a hand on James's thick-set shoulder. "Let's go."

The three of us make our way up the steps. Lando hasn't moved from his position on the sofa, except he's now hugging the boob cushion.

"Nice. Knew they'd come in handy." Miles chuckles.

"Lan, you need to sit up for takeoff." I try shaking him, but once Lando's asleep, it's easier to wake dead people, and that's before he's drunk half a bottle of whiskey. "Lando. Sit up, will you?"

The two stewards are fussing around in the galley, readying the plane. James has just removed the final cock balloon, and the cabin almost looks like normal.

I'm still trying to wake up my eldest brother. "Someone help, will you?"

Hendricks moves behind Lando, ready to hoist him up under his armpits, when he bolts upright.

"Lan, how're you doing?" he asks quietly.

Lando peers around the cabin. A look flashes across his face like he's wondering where he is and how the fuck he got here. Somehow, he manages to stand, but it's akin to watching a baby take its first steps before he drops into one of the seats.

"Lando?"

"Well, I was supposed to be getting married and instead I'm on a plane with my three younger brothers."

"Sounds like a bloody good change of plans to me."

I pin Miles with as stern a look as I can muster

and take the seat next to Lando. "Milo…"

"Sorry…" he replies, not sounding sorry in the slightest, "but you've had a lucky escape. We all know it, and you know it."

"Miles, give it a rest. Just for today, okay?"

"Your Grace, my lords, everything's set," James announces as he re-enters the cabin. "Your luggage is in the back. A car will be waiting for you upon arrival at Aspen airport, and we're in contact with Mr. Williams's team—the house will be open and ready for you. And there's a car in the garage for you to use at your disposal."

I smile up at him; there's literally nothing the man can't do.

"Thanks, James," everyone cries, except Lando, who's facedown on the boob cushion.

"One last thing, my lord. The press office has drawn up a press release for you…" He opens the thick leather folder wedged under his arm and passes me a piece of paper. "Perhaps"—he glances at Lando's head—

"you could sign it off?"

I scan over it.

Orlando Burlington, the eleventh Duke of Oxfordshire, and Caroline Montegue have regretfully decided…blah blah blah…love and support for one another…blah blah blah…they thank everyone…blah blah blah…

"Thanks, James, looks fine to me." I pass it back to him. "Sorry we're leaving you with all the shit to deal with."

"Plus, Clemmie and Mum," mumbles Miles.

"It's what I do best." James smiles sincerely, before exiting the cabin with a "See you in a week."

Five minutes of safety checks and taxiing later, the front wheels lift from the runway. There's a sigh of relief as we speed through the gray London clouds until it's impossible to tell where we are, except on the plane, leaving the mess behind.

"Okay." Miles claps his hands together. "We all need a drink, then you two are going to explain to Hendricks and me why the fuck we're on a plane over the English Channel instead of walking down the aisle next to some of the hottest bridesmaids I've ever seen."

"Not that we're not relieved at the turn of events, mind you."

I nod in agreement to Hendricks, before my eyes flick to Lando and back to the twins, who are eagerly waiting for an explanation. I'm suddenly filled with gratitude at the urgency with which my brothers responded to the *no-questions-asked* message I sent on the family group chat telling them the wedding was off and to meet us at the plane.

"Drinks first."

"Maybe not such a large one for the duke," mutters Hendricks, thumbing to the mop of Lando's hair, which is all we can make out until he lifts his head.

Pushing his sunglasses up, we're greeted with his very bloodshot, formerly Burlington-blue eyes; the anger and hurt palpable to all of us. "Look," he croaks, "before we start on everything, can I just say one thing?"

"Sure."

"Thank you, thank you for getting me out of there."

Miles jumps up from his seat and wraps him in a hug. As annoying as he is, our baby brother is the biggest softy to anyone in his orbit, and tears are his kryptonite. "It's okay, Lan, we got you."

"Thanks, Milo. I appreciate it."

By the time the stewards have delivered a round of drinks and brought some much-needed snacks, Lando is looking slightly less worse for wear.

"Lan? You want to begin?"

He waits until the cabin is just the four of us and lifts the glass to his lips, only to put it down again without drinking.

"Last night, I went over to Bluebell Cottage, where Caroline was staying before the wedding. I wanted to see her one last time…" This time when he picks up his glass, he downs the contents in one without so much as a wince. "I found her screwing someone."

I watch the twins for their reaction, because I'm expecting something, *anything*, but they sit there passively, and I'm sure I catch Hendricks side-eye Miles, but I blink and he's staring at Lando again.

"Tell them who it was," I say quietly.

"Jeremy."

"Jeremy?" spits Miles. "Jeremy Glenroths?"

I nod.

"What the fuck?! Lando!" they shout in sync.

This is the reaction I'd originally been expecting, not that Lando notices anything unusual. He's too drunk, steadily becoming more so since he found his fiancée and best friend in bed. Or, more accurately, against the wall.

"Hang on," Hendricks interrupts before Miles gets there first. "If this was last night, why are we only on a plane now? Why are we only finding out now?"

I look at my watch. "Because I only found out approximately four hours ago. We were meeting for a morning ride, and I discovered him like this in Thunder's stable. Drunk and fully dressed."

Miles's gaze goes from me to Lando and back again as something dawns on him. His mouth drops. "Don't tell me you were still going to marry her?"

Lando looks down into his empty glass, turning it round and round in his fingers.

"Lan!?"

"What was I supposed to do?" Lando snarls, though it's more of a slurry snarl. He clenches his fist, highlighting the cuts and faint bruises across his knuckles. "The entire country is watching this wedding."

"Um…not marry her." Miles rolls his eyes straight up to the clouds, like it's that easy. "Who gives a fuck how many people are watching?"

"Spoken like a true little brother."

Before Miles can tell Lando he's too weighed

down by his responsibilities as the duke, which is what got him into this mess with Caroline in the first place, Hendricks slaps a hand over his mouth. Because if we've heard this argument—the one where Miles doesn't know the meaning of responsibility, and Lando's got a stick up his arse—once, we've heard it a thousand times.

"So what happened?"

I shrug. "I told him he wasn't marrying Caroline. And made some calls."

It's a very rough summary of events. But I don't have the energy right now to go into how I found Lando slumped against the wall of the stables and blathering on to his favorite horse. We would have left sooner if it hadn't taken me an hour to understand what he was saying.

"Do Mum and Clemmie know the full story?"

I shake my head. "We'll tell them once Lando's sobered up. They just know the wedding is off. Did you see Mum?"

"We did, when we went back to pick up the snowboard," says Hendricks.

"And..."

Hendricks's mouth is doing that thing where he's trying really hard not to laugh. "I think she's relieved you didn't propose with Granny's ring."

Even Lando smiles at that, not that he found it funny at the time, because Caroline wanted a *new diamond* not a dusty old stone, regardless of whether it was a priceless, seven-carat, antique-cut diamond ring that had once belonged to Anne Boleyn. In fact, I almost feel sorry for Caroline. *Almost,* because once the Duchess of Oxfordshire finds out what really happened, she will have to deal with her wrath.

If beheading were still a thing, Caroline would be marched straight to the guillotine. Just as the ring's original owner had.

As though Lando senses this, he turns to me with a grateful, if solemn, expression. "So, what's the plan then?"

"Called in a favor. Murray Williams has lent us his Aspen place for the week," I reply, mentioning one of my best friends. "We're going to distract ourselves with a fuck load of freshly fallen snow."

"We're going skiing?"

My heart squeezes tight at the look of gratitude on Lando's face. That one look tells me he knows how desperate I was to get him out of England. I never ski before Christmas. It's far too fucking Christmassy. I don't have the heart to tell him that in all the hurry of getting us out of the country to faraway refuge, I'd forgotten that Aspen isn't the place to go if you want to avoid Christmas. Too late now.

"Al…" he whispers, and I'm forcing the ball of tears back down my throat, though thankfully the moment's lost when Miles pumps his fist in the air.

"Can't wait. I fucking love Aspen, and I love pre-Christmas skiing. Maybe I'll get some snow polo in." He tilts his head at me with a curious quirk of his eyebrow. "Al, does this mean you won't be quite the miserable Grinch you usually are this time of year?"

The temperature in the cabin drops significantly, or it might just be me.

"I'm not miserable, I just hate December."

"Dad loved December," Miles reminds me unnecessarily.

"I *know*."

"He'd hate that you were like this."

"Enough, Miles!" Lando almost shouts.

Wisely, Miles stays silent. It's not the first time he's brought up our father's love for Christmas, it won't be the last. But I definitely don't want to hear it today. Not that I ever do.

As if sensing my descending mood, Hendricks bangs his hands on the table. "It's the Burlington brothers together again. This week's going to be amazing."

"Can't fucking wait. Aspen has no idea what it's letting itself in for," adds Miles as the plane begins swaying through a thick cloud, and Lando erupts from his seat.

"I'm gonna be sick."

He makes it to the bathroom before the retching echoes out, which I should probably take as a sign that—Christmas or not, called-off wedding or not—this trip isn't going to be a total disaster.

Merry Christmas

Haven

2

I push through the doors to The Old Saloon, which are, ironically, really heavy, but Joe says it's to keep the tourists out.

Not that he's very successful in doing that, or *wants* to do it. He likes to act the grump, but really he loves how much his bar is loved, because if you've been to Aspen enough times, you know The Old Saloon is one of the best places for après-ski.

A *hidden gem, Condé Nast Traveler* once called it.

Joe thinks it's because all the Europeans

have been watching too many American cowboy programs on the TV and want to experience old-timey America. I *know* it's because of his wife's eggnog—once you taste it, there's no way you're not coming back for more. Famous around here because of its secret recipe, no one knows what she puts in it, even Joe, but she swears it cures you of all illness, and I've never seen anything to suggest otherwise.

Getting a fever—*Martha's eggnog*. Sinus infection, headache, chills—*Martha's eggnog*. Don't want to hit the slopes today? Get some of that eggnog down you, girl, and clip into those skis.

My theory is there's enough bourbon in it to start a bonfire if you hold a match too close, therefore one glass and any germs within a fifty-yard radius are killed by the fumes. But hey, that's just me.

Most of the locals from around here take it up the mountain in a hip flask. At least if you don't get down safely, you're too drunk to notice.

Shaking myself clear of the snow falling

outside, I hang my jacket on the rack by the entrance and look around. The fire blazing in the center grate is creating enough warmth to have the windows steamed up. It's busy. Almost every table is full with patrons in various stages of skiing undress—cozy knits, thick jackets, fur-lined boots—all screaming *money, money, money.*

Because that's what Aspen's about. For most people.

"Haven!" Joe shouts over the Christmas rock 'n' roll and heavy chatter as he spots me sneaking past the bar, hoping not to be noticed. "What time d'you call this?"

Dang it.

"Um…five?" I reply, knowing full well what the time is and why he's wearing an expression of annoyance. Even more so than usual, not that I ever take it seriously. Joe's bark is way worse than his bite.

"Yeah. Five. So how come I'm only seeing you for the first time today?"

I move into a space in the middle of the bar left by a group of guys taking their drinks, and I lean over the counter.

"You know I had to go to the bank today. I didn't have time for lunch, I'm sorry."

His face softens, and one bushy eyebrow shoots up as he watches me flail about, my hand moving blindly under the counter trying to find the jar of spicy crackers I know is always here. Except it's not there.

"Looking for these?" he asks, removing the missing jar from the shelf behind him and sliding it over the smooth wooden bar top into my waiting hands.

I grin sheepishly and pop the top. Just like the eggnog, these crackers are Martha's secret and arguably more addictive. In fact, maybe they *do* have crack in them. They're that addictive. Probably best not to ask.

He peers at me, watching me shove a handful into my mouth. "Don't tell me that's the first thing you've eaten all day?"

I shake my head, because it's true. I did eat today. I had a cinnamon bun followed by a gingerbread house I'd broken.

Not the most nutritious breakfast, but I haven't had time for anything else, including lunch, which I have here every day without fail—except today, obviously. Not sure Joe believes me though, considering I'm inhaling the crackers so quickly they've barely touched the sides.

"There's a chicken schnitzel waiting on the table with Saylor. But you know if you see Martha, tell her you had it at lunchtime." He winks. "Or I'll never hear the end of it about not feeding you properly. Not that you're not a grown woman an' all."

I push up on the bar so I can kiss his cheek. "I love you, Joe."

"Go and eat something."

Moving through the crowds, ducking underneath the huge tray laden with empty glasses, which Mike, one of the Saloon servers, is carrying, I spot my best friend sitting at our usual table over in the corner, and breathe a sigh of relief.

"Hey." I drop down in the booth seat opposite her, head falling back on the plush leather surround, and finally let the weariness of the day take over.

Probably should have had lunch.

"You look exhausted." Saylor points out the obvious.

"I am."

"Well, what happened? How'd it go?" she asks right as she slides out of the booth and runs off in the direction of the kitchens, only to return thirty seconds later carrying a plate with what I know is my lunch five hours too late. "I was instructed to make sure you ate this as soon as you arrived."

Even the sight of it has my mouth watering. The thinnest breadcrumbed chicken and a giant heap of mashed potatoes stare up at me. I can't pick up my fork quickly enough.

"Omigawdsohungry," I manage to garble

around the first mouthful before going back in for the second. "Dyoueat?"

Saylor blinks as she tries to figure out what I've just said.

"Did you eat yet?" I ask, picking up a glass of water I assume is mine, to rinse the two huge mouthfuls I inhaled.

"That was here when I sat down."

I just about manage to stop the splutter erupting from me, but not Saylor's grin erupting from *her*.

"Kidding. It's yours. Poured fresh by me, and yes, I did eat when I got here *an hour ago*." Her eyebrow lifts pointedly, because I was also supposed to be here an hour ago.

"Sorry—"

"It's fine, gave me a chance to scope out the visiting hotties. There are some good ones in here tonight." She finishes her assessment of the bar and its patrons and turns to me. "It's December now, and I think we need to start having a little fun. You definitely need a fling or two this Christmas."

My mouth is too full to respond, which Saylor takes as a sign to steamroll right through.

"You haven't had sex with anyone since that guy in the summer, right? I haven't hooked up with anyone since Halloween. We need to rectify it, Havey, it's too long. Let's make this holiday a memorable one."

"I don't have time for fun." I scoop up a forkful of mashed potato.

"That's not true…"

"Hey, do you want to hear about my day or not?

Sitting forward, I pull out the rolled-up file I've had wedged into the back of my jeans. Saylor takes it and removes the thick wad of papers I've been carrying around most of the day. All different documents, all pertaining to my life in some way, and *all* telling me what I'm too nervous to believe could be true.

The disaster of my life for the past four years is almost over, and I can start to rebuild. Or simply *start.*

"How did the meetings go?"

"As well as I could have hoped." I shrug.

"And the business—"

"It will be fully mine once the remaining debt is paid off."

"Shiiit." She hisses out, her vowels elongating because Saylor also can't believe I'm quite there.

Everyone in this town knows my dad died. Only Saylor, Joe, and Martha know that the reason I've been busting my ass for the four years since, was to pay off the sixty-plus grand in medical expenses he left me, which the insurance didn't cover.

Money I did *not* have.

Out of habit, I glance over at the wall of photos running down the side of the bar, homing in on the one of my dad with his arm around Joe, his best friend. If you're close enough, you can just about make out a ten-year-old me, in the far background next to some freshly planted saplings.

During the winter, my dad, Wyatt Wylder, was the guy you came to if you wanted the biggest and best Christmas tree. Through the trees grown on our land, bordered by the national forest, he supplied the hotels and restaurants in the area, plus all the local ski lodges and private homes being prepared for demanding holiday guests. We also owned a tree store—yes, store—which my mom had started, where you can buy anything you need for decorating at Christmas, plus the tree.

In the summer he was no less busy.

All the trees cut through the winter made way for new saplings to be planted and grown over the following years. In the peak months he would take out guided trips to Talisker Summit, a flat stretch of the Rocky Mountains range on the edge of our land. A perfect setup for campfires and star gazing, from which you could see miles and miles of Colorado's mountains and Aspen's valley far below. He'd talk and talk, telling tales of old Aspen, about the magic of the town and how you could still find silver if you looked hard enough.

I first noticed my dad was sick five years ago. He wasn't waking up quite so early, he was tired more easily, and it was taking him longer to cut the trees. It turned out he'd known a good while more than that. He'd known he was getting sick, and instead of asking for help when he could, he decided he needed to protect me, until it was too late. My blood still boils when I think about it. Think of all the time we lost together, because he thought I couldn't cope with more bad news so soon after my mom died.

The upshot? After he passed, I discovered he'd been juggling my mom's medical bills by downgrading his own care and, as his sole next of kin, once his life insurance was paid out, it was up to me to cover the shortfall.

What I also hadn't realized until my father died, is how coveted our small piece of land is. Seven hundred acres of prime Aspen real estate. The vultures circled, offering huge sums of money, but even when I'd cry myself to sleep wondering how I would ever pay the bills, I knew that I'd never sell the ranch. If he hadn't while he was alive, there's no way I'd sell it now he was dead.

My dad had built the house from scratch. It was where I'd been born. It was where my mom's ashes were scattered next to the tree under which Mr. Frosty, our Newfoundland, was buried. It was my history. All twenty-five years of it, and if I ever met someone and had a kid, I would want them to grow up with the same experience.

By some miracle, I'd kept hold of it.

Four winters of selling trees. Four summers of taking tourists camping every day and saving my tips. Along with waiting tables in the evenings, and working the counter of Aspen's famous bakery, serving coffees to the pre-ski morning crowd, I have almost paid off everything.

The pile of papers on the table in front of me is proof.

I spent the day in meetings with the bank

manager, the insurance representatives, and the mortgage guy, all of whom told me the same thing.

"I have seven grand left to pay. And I could make that in tips alone if I get a few good tables this holiday." Aspen's clientele is generous, if nothing else.

"And then Wylder Ranch becomes Haven's Holistic Yoga Retreat or whatever we're calling it?"

I chuckle, picking up the water, wishing it was something stronger. I need something stronger. "Nah, I think it'll always be Wylder Ranch. For the holidays anyway."

"But yoga for the summer?"

"We'll see how it goes." I shrug. "It might be a disaster."

Two years ago, I took a lady up to Talisker Summit. It had been a quiet weekday trip, just her and me. She'd come from L.A., where she owned yoga and Pilates studios. As soon as we'd reached the flat ground, she'd rolled out her yoga mat and proclaimed it to be the most beautiful view she'd ever seen.

I'd joined her on the ground, and she'd guided me through a practice.

Hand on my heart I could honestly say that afterward, sitting there looking down at the valley, two years of stress and grief released from me. I cried for a solid two hours.

Professional? Absolutely not.

But on the way back, the lady had asked if I'd ever be interested in running yoga retreats up there. Specifically, *her* retreats. It was a perfect space, she'd said. No cell reception. No disturbances. Just the earth and sky, and a whole lot of stars.

She'd left me her business card, and I'd stared at it every day for a year before I finally decided to call her up and ask her what the retreat would entail. Long story short, this summer, Wylder Ranch is hosting its very first yoga weekend.

"I think yoga people are way too chill to have disasters," Saylor shot back. And if it wasn't obvious, Saylor Anderson is a big supporter of any plans that get me living my own life.

"Okay, I need more than water." I stand, picking up my empty plate to drop into the kitchen. "You want a beer or eggnog?"

"Beer. Otherwise, you'll be peeling me off the floor."

"Lightweight." I grin.

"Yeah, that's why you love me."

"Yeah, yeah," I call over my shoulder.

After saying a quick hi to the guys in the kitchens, and stealing a fry from the hot pans, I make my way to the bar. Even in the thirty minutes I've been sitting down, it's now so busy there are no spare tables. The space running down the left of the bar where the pool table is housed is also full. It's getting hot. Sweaty hot.

I'm peeling off my sweater when I notice a guy standing next to the jukebox, staring at it like it ate his last quarter, and I swear he's about to kick it. But that's not what has me detouring over there, because that goddamn jukebox needs to be kicked on the regular.

No, ma'am.

It's the low-slung black jeans that does it. The ones hugging thick thighs and a firm, rounded ass, and tucked into a pair of worn leather brown boots that look like they've been pulled on in a hurry, given the way the laces are hanging loose. It's also the cozy knit sweater he's wearing—the unofficial uniform around here, except this one has me wanting to reach out and touch it. See if it's as soft and cozy as it looks, stretched across a broad back and even broader shoulders.

He's the epitome of Aspen clientele, but at the same time set so far apart from everyone else in here I can't look away. He scrubs both hands through his light brown hair, and the way he tugs on the ends has me quickening my step.

"You okay there?"

My entire core clenches. Deep blue eyes briefly flash to mine before returning to the offering in front of him. His left hand grips the edges of the jukebox, and the neon light flashing along the sides catches the large gold signet ring sitting askew on his pinkie.

I grasp my fists and fight the urge to straighten it. Or run my fingers through his hair.

Jesus. Saylor was right. It's been far too long since I've had sex.

"It's all Christmas music."

I pause, because that's not what I was expecting him to say, because, *duh,* it's Christmas. I also wasn't expecting the accent, which definitely isn't American. Though, given how he looks like he fell out of a Ralph Lauren "quintessential Englishman" ad, I probably shouldn't be too surprised.

"It's the holidays. What did you want? Slipknot?"

He scoffs out a thick, gravelly laugh, and through the light five-o'clock shadow covering his cheeks, I see deep dimples pull in. *Shit.* This guy's as hot from the front as his ass suggests.

"Christ, no..." he begins, then stops. "Wait, you're not a fan, are you? I'm not about to dig myself a hole am I, and insult you?"

I slowly shake my head. "They're a little shouty for my taste."

"Oh good, me too." He turns back to the jukebox and huffs as the pages flick. "All bloody Christmas.

"Since you're not after festive music, or Slipknot, what are you looking for?"

"Literally, anything else."

I realize I'm hanging on to every word he says because even the most boring words, like *literally*—that pop of the *T*—sound goddamn amazing when they drop from his very full lips.

LIT-RALeee.

I close my mouth before I drool all over him and check over my shoulder to make sure no one's looking. Stepping in next to him, I punch in a code that brings up the music selection Joe uses for the other eleven months of the year, and flick through until I find what I need.

"I can only offer you Michael Bublé, I'm afraid. But it's enough that most people in here—including Joe—won't notice it's been switched."

"Excellent, I can live with Michael Bublé. Thank you very much." The hottie flashes a toothy, almost heart-stopping, white smile. And my eyes focus on those dimples again. "But who's Joe?"

"He owns the place." I nod over to the bar, where Joe is currently yelling something at Mike. "And he *loves* Christmas."

Hottie taps a long index finger to the side of his nose. "Got it, it'll stay our little secret."

It's all I can manage to smile back, instead of gawp like I want to.

Yup. I really need to have sex.

Four years of working to pay off my parents' debts has left me very little time to myself. I mostly flop onto my bed every night, exhausted, occasionally reaching into my bedside drawer for one of my battery-operated friends if I haven't already fallen asleep. I don't have time to date, but

I have had the occasional hookup with a tourist, because it's easy and feelings don't get in the way.

But, as Saylor reminded me, it's been too long since I did that either.

That's why my mouth's pooling with saliva, and I'm having to force myself to blink.

Not just because this man in front of me is the hottest guy I've ever seen in my life. Aspen is full of hot guys, especially at this time of year when they're all wrapped up in cable knit like a present waiting to be opened.

"Thank you." This time I force myself to step away before I do something really embarrassing.

"No, thank *you* for saving me from listening to Christmas music for longer than I need to."

One more step back. There, *this* is a much safer distance. "You're welcome."

"So, you're local I take it, seeing as you know the jukebox trick, and Joe the owner. Any recommendations on what to do while I'm here?"

"Yeah, make sure you try the eggnog," I call over my shoulder.

Merry Christmas

Merry Christmas

Alexander

3

That *fucking* eggnog.

I groan, unstick my tongue from the roof of my mouth, and somehow manage to roll myself to the side of the bed where I know there's water.

Hydration. I need hydration. Gulping down the entire glass, I push myself up on my elbow and ease into a full sitting position. My brain gives one hard thump inside my skull, then stops.

God knows what time it is.

God knows what time my body *thinks* it is.

Shards of dim light peek out of the huge curtains, so it must be near morning, but that's the only clue. I brave turning my head and prepare myself for the onslaught of pain. Any…second… now.

My entire body curls in on itself as my brain tries to escape my skull, without success. My lungs seize in shock, my breath traps in my throat somewhere while it rides the excruciating agony searing through me.

I'm *never* drinking again.

I might say that every time I'm hungover. But this time, I mean it.

What even is eggnog anyway? *Fucking* eggnog.

I'm still trying to focus on my surroundings when I finally spy my watch on the side table, next to my phone. Seven a.m. That makes it sometime after lunch back home. It's enough to stop me from reaching for my phone, because I know full well that I'll open it to a barrage of messages about escaping England, and I'm far too hungover to deal with that.

The banging in my head dies down enough for me to make out the unmistakable smell of coffee, and it's all I need to power myself forward and out of bed. Carefully, of course.

First coffee. Then painkillers.

Pulling on a pair of fleecy pajama pants and the one hoodie Miles so generously packed for me, I follow the scent along a dimly lit corridor and down the stairs to the cabin's cavernous main room. Someone's been busy. There's already a roaring fire crackling in the wide stone fireplace dividing the center and an enormous Christmas tree twinkling away at the far end, which I do my best to ignore, but that's not what has me stopping in my tracks.

It's the wall of windows.

Bloody hell.

By the time we arrived yesterday afternoon, a blizzard was whipping up the air, so we saw nothing more than a hazy, gray landscape. But this morning…

It's almost enough to banish this hangover.

Crisp, freshly fallen snow covers everything in sight.

A vast panorama of white, surrounded by mountain tops looking down on a wide river. In the distance the sun has just broached the horizon, turning the ground a deep orange. Trees give way to the thick mounds of snow and their branches bounce back green and clean. The view is only broken up by a few other cabins dotting along the edge of the valley, and chimney smoke curls in the air before disappearing into what promises to be a stunning day.

Directly below me, past the veranda with an enormous firepit and seating for at least twenty, is a covered pool and an equally large hot tub I'll be trying out later.

Even though I'd say it's worth every penny of the seventy-five mil, or whatever Murray paid for it, it's only the second most beautiful place I've ever been. Nothing will ever beat the views from Burlington Hall—our family home for the past five hundred years— and its fifteen thousand acres of Oxfordshire countryside, including the village of Valentine Nook.

The noise of a door being flung open has me turning around to find Hendricks and Miles marching in. One of the more annoying qualities my younger brothers have—and there are *many*—is their ability to function after a night of drinking and display little to no evidence of a hangover. The pair of them had more to drink than Lando and me combined—including Lando's twenty-four-hour binge—yet they look like they've just walked out of the spa my mother frequents every month, Burlington-blue eyes clear and sparkling with the ever-present mischief.

"Oh good, you're up," says Hendricks, yanking off his beanie and shaking it free of snow, before closing the door behind him.

I study them as they walk toward me. Maybe they've not been to bed. Still being drunk would account for that identical grin plastered across both their faces.

Miles pauses midstride. "What?"

"*How* are you two up?"

"Jet lag is for the weak."

"Screw jet lag. You had more of that eggnog than Lando and I did. Why aren't you hungover?"

Hendricks shrugs, while Miles drops down in the chair opposite me, shucks off his jacket, and tosses it onto one of the empty chairs, then props his feet on the table. "That stuff was delicious. Need to get the recipe so we can take it back to Burlington."

Over my dead body. Though any more of that, and I probably would be dead.

"How amazing is this place?" Miles continues, either ignoring the way I'm staring at him, or he hasn't noticed in the first place. Probably the latter. "We should buy one."

"We have a ski chalet." I remind him.

"But that's in Switzerland. We should buy one here. I always forget how awesome the skiing is, and it'll mean I can spend more time here for polo in the summer. It would be a great investment. We can find somewhere with land and build stables…"

Given our current view, I'm certainly tempted. But I've already stopped listening because it's Lando's problem. As the head of this family, all financial investments fall to our eldest brother, therefore Miles will thankfully have to talk to *him* about it. My head is still banging far too much to enter into a conversation about property.

"So, where've you been already?"

"We drove into the town, but nothing was open. Milo wanted to go to the polo club but then decided he was too hungry, so we had to come back," Hendricks replies.

Just the mention of Miles being hungry has my own stomach rumbling. This house would normally be fully staffed, but considering we arrived with little to no notice, I wasn't expecting James to organize something quite so quickly.

"What are we going to do for breakfast? I need painkillers."

"Maggie's making it."

My brow furrows—even *that* hurts. I might have been drunk last night, but I *know* we didn't bring any girls back. And there's *no way* Miles has picked someone up before seven a.m. even if it was to make breakfast.

"Who the hell's Maggie?"

"John, the house manager, sent her over. Hen and I met her this morning."

I scratch my head and curse the eggnog again. I'm usually much better at this. "So, it wasn't you two who made coffee this morning?"

Miles's laugh is all I need as an answer.

I'm wondering how I'm going to get this coffee I can smell, along with painkillers I'm becoming more desperate for by the second, plus this breakfast when, as if by magic, a woman appears through a door in the far corner I hadn't noticed before. She's carrying a loaded tray of cups and a huge pot of coffee. Leaping up to help her, I'm rewarded with a piercing bolt of pain right between the eyes.

"Good morning. Breakfast is set in the dining room, if you're hungry. Or I can bring it in here for you," she announces, moving the tray out of my reach before I can help her because Miles gets there first.

I'd roll my eyes if I didn't think it would cause me another shot of pain, because from the way she's looking at him, I'm beginning to think maybe Miles *has* picked someone up this morning.

"Thanks, darling." He winks and Maggie's cheeks immediately turn an impressive shade of beetroot. "And you couldn't rustle up a few Advil, could you?"

By the time she returns with a full bottle, I'm ready to dunk my head in a foot of snow to freeze out the banging.

Fucking eggnog.

It takes double-strength painkillers, almost the entire pot of coffee, a stack of pancakes with the best maple syrup I've ever tasted, along with scrambled eggs and bacon before I begin to feel remotely human again.

Hendricks is on FaceTime with his three-year-old son and Miles is scrolling through his phone on the opposite end of the sofa I'm trying to snooze on.

"That was some quick thinking yesterday, Al. Every news outlet has led with it. Clemmie said half the press are camping outside the Burlington gates because they think Lando is there, and the other half are in The Cupid's Arrow trying to find out what happened from anyone in Valentine Nook who'll talk to them."

"I know," I mumble, without bothering to

open my eyes. "I'm on the group text."

"Mum said she'll send James out with a shotgun if they don't all leave soon."

"I know," I repeat. "I'm on the group text."

"And Clem—"

My eyes fly open. "Milo, are you going to give me a rundown of everything I already know because I'm. On. The. Group. Text?"

He sighs heavily. "Just making conversation. You're so grumpy."

"I'm tired and hungover."

"Well, as soon as Hen's off the phone we have plans that will perk you right up. You did the hard work getting us here, so Henners and I have appointed ourselves activity monitors."

This gets my attention. I'm very well accustomed to Hendricks and Miles's activities—some of which may or may not have landed them an invite to spend the night in our local jail cell from time to time. Even if it is the Valentine Nook jail cell, which *technically* our family owns.

"What does that mean?"

"It means we're about to have fun. We're waking Lando, then we're going to get our Christmas tree, and we'll hit the slopes before lunch."

The words are out of my mouth before my brain has time to catch up. "I'm not going to pick a tree."

Miles pins me with his rarely seen but very firm glare. "Yes. You are."

"Milo, don't start."

"Alex, this week isn't about you, it's about Lando. And we're going to get a tree to decorate."

His tone is daring me to challenge him, and I can already tell from the look in his eye this will turn into a blaring argument if I let it. Miles might be the biggest softy of the Burlington family, but he's equally stubborn, loyal to a fault, and holds a grudge like no one I've ever met. He will also go on and on *and on* about it until I give in.

Unfortunately, he's right.

This week isn't about me. It'll be much easier all around if I set aside my aversion to Christmas and everything that goes along with it, and just do what Miles wants in a bid to make sure Lando's okay.

"We don't have any decorations," is the only argument I can muster at one last futile attempt to get out of doing something I have point-blank refused to do since I was twelve years old. "And we already have a tree." I point to the one flashing haphazardly in the corner.

"Maggie is sorting us out with decorations. We're going to pick the tree this morning, and we're going to spend the afternoon decorating it."

The familiar panic swirls in my gut. "Milo…please."

Miles sits up and glares at me. My pleading has no effect.

"No, Al. Not this year. Enough is enough. It's been twenty years, and Dad would hate it. He would *hate* you were like this. And Lando always feels too guilty to push you, but he hates it too. We *all* hate you're like this. No one blames you *except you*. Do it for Lando."

I stay silent.

Lando rarely mentions my aversion to Christmas, or the fact that I usually disappear in December, only to resurface for one day before leaving again. He's never pushed me on it. Not like Miles, and Hendricks, or my mum. Or even Clemmie. He never says anything because I know my guilt eats at him too.

Lando became the eleventh Duke of Oxfordshire the day our father died. He was fourteen years old. I was twelve.

Along with the title, Lando inherited approximately six hundred thousand acres of land across the United Kingdom, Europe, Asia, and North America, as well as business holdings in property, technology, sustainability, and roughly nine billion pounds cash.

Up until he was eighteen, our father's

advisors helped run Burlington Estate Group Limited, which was set up by the first Duke of Oxfordshire in 1511. But once he legally became an adult, the responsibilities of keeping our family together fell onto his shoulders.

Something he wasn't quite ready for, because if it hadn't been for me, he wouldn't have inherited the title so early.

If it hadn't been for me, our father would still be alive.

It was a rainy Saturday two weeks before Christmas.

Lando and I had come home from boarding school for the Christmas holidays. One of our traditions had always been to decorate the Christmas tree as a family—it was what I was looking forward to the most. It was the most beautiful tree—big and twinkling—and once the star was placed on the top, it almost touched the ceiling of the great hall at Burlington. After the tree was decorated, we would watch a Christmas movie as a family.

with popcorn, and we'd be allowed to stay up late. It was my most treasured time.

The twins were only six at that point, and Clemmie was still a baby, and when Lando and I returned home, instead of a naked tree waiting for us to be decorated, the lights were on, the branches weighed down with ornaments—even the ones with my name on them—and the star was shining on top. It had been decided the tree would go up early, and instead of watching a movie, we were going to the pantomime.

I can still feel the disappointment burning in my chest.

I was a twelve-year-old boy, tired from a long term at school, looking forward to seeing my parents and decorating the Christmas tree. I didn't want to go to the pantomime.

I cried, stormed up to my room, and refused to go out. When I was still upset the next morning, my inherently kind dad decided to go out and get another tree for us all to decorate. Just like we always did.

He never came home.

Driving around the corner of a notoriously dangerous country lane, a tractor had been coming toward him on the opposite side of the road. The driver *behind* the tractor, impatient at the ten miles an hour it was traveling, decided to overtake. He never saw my dad's Range Rover and went headfirst into it. They were both killed instantly.

Next week will be the twentieth anniversary of his death.

I can reason that the accident wasn't my fault.

Miles is right. No one blames me but me. In fact, everyone else in my family still loves Christmas the way my dad loved Christmas. They celebrate it in his memory. They celebrate December.

It's something I wish I could do, but I can't.

Because I know that if it hadn't been for me, then my dad wouldn't have been driving to collect another tree at that precise moment in time, and he'd still be alive.

My mum would still have a husband, the twins and Clemmie would still have a father they spent time with instead of one they only remember through photos, and Lando would have been able to enjoy his teenage years without worrying about how to run an international multi-billion-pound company before he was ready.

So, yeah, that's why I hate Christmas.

"Fine. *For Lando*." I reply eventually, but refrain from telling him I'd much rather build a snowman. Honestly, I'm surprised that neither of the twins has suggested it. Snowmen, snowballs, and snow fights are the twins' vibe. "When are we going?"

"As soon as Lando's awake."

I balk. I know full well if I walk into Lando's bedroom and tell him we're going Christmas tree shopping, he will quite rightly tell me to fuck off. It's the twins' idea. They can deal with what could most certainly be compared to waking a bear during hibernation.

Add a hangover the size of Texas, and you could very well be in perilous danger.

"I'm not doing it."

"Neither am I," Miles shoots back just as quickly and shudders dramatically. But then his voice softens. "Do you think he'll remember what's happened?"

"Yes," I reply, though the thought briefly occurred to me that we'd have to remind him.

"Do you know if he's spoken to Caroline yet?"

I shake my head.

"What a fucking twenty-four hours."

And that's all there is to say, because *what a fucking twenty-four hours,* and I finally get to close my eyes for a few minutes peace, until we both sense Hendricks's presence.

"What?" he says, shutting his phone off to find Miles and me staring at him.

I return his confusion with the smile I

know I'm going to have to wear all day. Better get the practice in. "You've been nominated to wake up the duke."

His jaw clenches and he summons a deep breath, but his groan is heard with every step to Lando's bedroom.

Alexander

4

Downtown Aspen is like Christmas drank too much Christmas cheer and then threw it up.

It's how I imagine a Hallmark movie set would look on the most Christmassy movie ever. Even poor Chanel, with its classic black and white branding, has been wrapped up like a present. There's a light dusting of snow falling, making me feel like I'm in the middle of a snow globe,

plus twinkly lights causing my eye to twitch, a live Christmas jazz band that's not helping my headache, and a light-up Santa on his sleigh pulled by eight reindeer.

It's all here. There's nothing forgotten.

It's perfect. If you like that sort of thing.

I want to go back to bed and hide until January. Instead, I grit my teeth and plaster on my best smile. *For Lando.*

"Okay, boys. What type of tree are we getting." Miles rubs his hands together with a level of glee I've never been able to reach at any time of year.

"A green one?" I reply.

Next to me, Lando chuckles. It's a dark, gruff chuckle, but at least it's *something*. He hasn't said much in the hour it took us to get dressed and leave the house, but he doesn't look quite as murderous as he did yesterday. Or as drunk. The sadness is still there though. Maybe I should smile less.

I honestly thought he'd flat out refuse to get a tree, which would give me the perfect excuse to stay behind, but in a surprising turn of events, he thought it was a great idea. If you could take his *yeah, whatever* response as thinking it was great. Miles did, anyway.

"I think I like Aspen," he mutters.

"Don't say that too loudly. Miles wants to buy a cabin here."

"Hmm. Maybe."

I should have kept my mouth shut, although I suddenly catch a whiff of ginger and cinnamon filtering through the frosty air, and saliva pools under my tongue. Up ahead there's a pale pink storefront with two dancing gingerbread men wearing light-up waistcoats, who look like they're monitoring the long line of people weaving out of the shop and down the street. The least intimidating doormen ever.

It's easily the longest queue I've seen, reminiscent of Disney rides when little men carry signs that tell you there are still four hours to go before you reach the front.

"We drove past here this morning and the queue was double." Hendricks turns around to Lando and me, then nudges Miles. "We have to come early tomorrow. There must be something good inside if the queue is *that* long."

"I was too hungry to wait." Miles points to the end of the long row of stores. "There's the Christmas tree place."

The Christmas tree place is not what I was expecting. I thought it would be like the wooden fenced pen Mr. Giles sets up in our village of Valentine Nook every December first. It is, in fact, just another storefront; possibly the most Christmassy storefront, with huge wreaths hanging on the windows—big enough to decorate the gates at Burlington. More twinkling lights are wrapped around the panes, a dark green sign juts out from the brick and reads Wylder Trees, and a little gold bell hangs above the door.

I hadn't noticed on the approach, but the side of the store *is* penned in—just like Mr. Giles's. This is where all the trees are, separated according to size going all the way up to twenty feet. Snow from the blizzard yesterday is resting on branches, and with the way they're lined up, it feels like I'm peering into Narnia.

Every memory of my childhood—good and terrible—hits so hard my eyes immediately sting with the warning of tears.

I turn away before I allow any to fall.

Christmas is *the worst.*

"How high d'you think the ceiling is? Twenty feet, thirty?"

I swipe a hand under my nose. "Milo, we're not getting a twenty-foot tree."

"Why not? They deliver." He points to a sign that says exactly that.

"How are you going to reach the top?" Lando asks, sensibly.

"Not to mention we already have a giant tree in the main room," I snap, harder than I mean to, but I'm *not* decorating a twenty-foot tree. "Just get a regular-size tree, for fuck's sake."

"I'm going inside to get help," Hendricks calls behind him as he marches into the store, under an archway of holly and ivy that's twined with glitter-covered twigs. A bundle of mistletoe hangs in the middle.

My jaw twitches. Christmas Trees. Mistletoe. *Glitter.*

I turn to see Miles put his arm around Lando and guide him off, leaving me alone, literally standing in my worst nightmare. How long do I have to be here before I can go home and pretend Christmas doesn't exist?

I don't bother to catch up with them.

Miles is no doubt trying to convince Lando why we should invest in land here, while also persuading him to buy the biggest tree, like a festive dick-measuring contest. They're walking around, heads bent in a whisper, and every few seconds, they stop in front of one and peer up to its top, then down to its bottom, as though they're some kind of tree connoisseurs. I watch as Lando says something to Miles that has him throwing his head back with a roar of laughter, and for a split second he looks so like our dad that I can't breathe.

Blowing some warmth into my hands, I spot a bench to sit on while I wait for everyone. Spying a lone Christmas bauble hanging on a nearby branch, I watch it swing back and forth with each flick I give it. It's so hypnotizing I almost manage to forget the anxiety churning in my gut along with the lump in my throat.

"I've brought help."

I spin around to find Hendricks walking under the glitter mistletoe arch next to *the help*. The lump in my throat immediately vanishes.

I honestly wasn't sure if I imagined her in my drunken haze or if we'd actually met. Then I remember those vivid green eyes flashing at me in amusement as she told me to try the eggnog, just like they're flashing at me now.

It's almost the last thing I remember.

Fucking eggnog.

She pauses midstride before a smile stretches across her face and lights up every single one of her features, crinkling her cute button nose. The green eyes widen under a thick fan of sooty black lashes resting on rosy cheeks. They're so pink, round and perfect, it's as though someone's drawn them onto her.

Seriously, she is stunning.

"Oh, hello, again. The Slipknot fan…"

I jump to my feet. For no reason at all, my mouth drops. So does my gaze. It coasts down to her winter boot–clad feet and slowly back up. *Really* slowly. An apron is wrapped around her waist, accentuating the most incredible curves I've ever seen, full and luscious. She's an hourglass come to life. Most of her dark blonde hair is piled on top of her head and there's a pen sticking out of it, and maybe a bulldog clip, and perhaps a bit of that glittery branch stuck in a loose tendril.

It would probably be weird if I removed it, right?

My eyes dart to her face again before I tear them away and make the mistake of attempting to read the words on her apron. Except I need to peer closer to make out *Wylder Ranch* stitched across the front, before realizing I look like I'm staring at her boobs.

Not my fault. Shouldn't have the logo in the same bloody color, should she?

Christmas Tree green, just like her eyes.

And *Jesus,* what I wouldn't give to see those berry-red lips wrapped around my cock.

How is she even real? She looks like she should come with wings and sit on top of the tree. *I could give her something to sit on. Oh dear god. What the fuck is the matter with me?*

An inhale of cold air gets stuck in my throat, which I manage to cough away before I start choking.

"Um, do you two know each other?" Hendricks frowns as Miles and Lando return from their tree assessment.

I'm still staring at her too hard to answer, too jolted by my reaction, but when her eyes dart away, a look of confusion fogs her face. It's the same one everybody gets the first time they meet the twins.

"I'm the younger and better-looking one." Miles winks, before she can say anything.

It's his standard line, and I roll my eyes at Lando, who's mouthing the words. Another line we've heard a thousand times. It usually ends up with the girl giving him her number, but if Miles thinks he's getting one this time, he's sorely mistaken.

I saw her first.

"Milo, not now," snaps Hendricks, his finger flicking between me and the eggnog girl, who I can't seem to stop looking at. "I want to go back to this. Something's going on."

My audience of three are moving their heads back and forth between us. Whatever the something is, it's weird and hot. The air crackles around us.

"Look, Al's blushing," Miles announces to everyone and no one. The candy he unwrapped—which was, in fact, the crackle in the air—is thrown in his mouth.

Behind me, Lando snorts.

I hate my brothers. I hate Christmas.

"I have the worst hangover I can remember," I say finally. "And it's your fault."

Eggnog girl throws her head back with a laugh so loud and genuine I can't help but join in. I also want to hear it again.

"Martha's eggnog?"

"Yes—"

"How do you know about the eggnog?" Hendricks interrupts.

"She's the one who recommended we try it," I answer without breaking my gaze.

"That stuff was incredible. We need the recipe."

She shakes her head, annoyingly turning her attention to the twins. "No dice. That recipe lives and will die with Martha, I'm afraid."

"I'm happy with that arrangement," I reply, making her laugh again.

Yes.

Pushing her hands into the back pockets of her jeans, she rocks on her boots. I don't know if she's realized she's just pushed her boobs closer to me. Probably not wise to point out either.

I just need to stop wondering what they'd look like with my dick sliding between them.

Spectacular is my guess.

"So, you're looking for a tree? Is this one of your things to do this week?" She smiles, giving my brothers far too much ammunition.

Not that they need any, but the three of them are wearing identical grins that say I'm going to hear about it later. Miles's eyebrow has disappeared under his flop of hair.

I never thought to mention her to them, but it's clear this girl wasn't just someone recommending a drink.

Three heads, six sets of eyes, all track in sync and wait for my answer.

"Something like that."

"Okay…let me show you what we have." Her

eyes crinkle again as she laughs.

"Hang on," Miles says, blocking the way for anyone to get past. "Introductions first… that's Lando, I'm Miles, this is Hendricks…" He jabs his thumb toward each of them, then throws his arm over my shoulder and slaps my chest with his spare hand. "And this fine specimen of an English gentleman is Alexander. But I see you already know that."

Lando snorts again, louder this time. Miles is smiling like he's just won Olympic gold in smugness, and this girl's cheeks are definitely pinker than they were a second ago.

"Actually, we never got around to names. Just a mutual dislike of shouty music. I'm Haven Wylder." She lets out a giggle, and her gaze slices around the four of us before landing on me again, where it stays like she's trying to decide for herself if I *am* a fine specimen. "Welcome to Wylder Trees."

"It's Alex, just Alex," I say, shrugging Miles's arm off. "Hello, Haven. Please lead the way."

We all let her go first, but before Miles can follow, I grab his arm and hiss, "Stop being a dickhead" in his ear.

"But it's so fun," he claps back, hurrying after the rest of them.

Haven guides us through the makeshift forest as Miles and Lando direct her to whatever it was they'd seen on their earlier investigation. We stop in front of one that's thankfully what I deem a regular size, and not one that would take all week to decorate. I can't tell if I'm a little disappointed when Miles announces it's the one he wants, because it means we're done and I won't get to spend any more time in Haven's company.

"So, tree shopping today, what else do you have planned for the week?" Haven asks as I go inside the store to settle the bill because it gives me an excuse to spend more time with her.

Predictably, I'm followed closely by the twins, watching me like they're only missing popcorn.

I lift a shoulder, jerking my head to Hendricks and Miles. "These two are the cruise directors.

Lando and I are along for the ride."

"Tomorrow we're going heli-skiing," Hendricks replies, watching for my reaction.

Surprise flashes across my face. Surprise and delight. I fucking *love* heli-skiing. We all do. The rush of landing on a deserted mountaintop and whizzing down fresh powder is unmatched. It's one of my favorite memories I have of being with my dad, when he'd decided I was old enough and experienced enough to go with him.

It's still the best day of my life. Just me, Lando, and Dad in St. Moritz.

"Are we?"

Now *that* I can get on board with. Snow and mountains. Nothing fucking Christmassy about that. Just winter being winter.

"Yeah, don't worry. We're planning things with the Grinch in mind too."

My chest deflates.

Haven turns back to me, eyes bright in amusement, and she bites down a smile.

"Grinch?"

Miles drops his arm over my shoulder again. "Yeah, Al here hates Christmas."

For Lando. For Lando. For Lando, I repeat, while promising to also disown Miles.

I once again shrug his arm off.

"You *hate* Christmas?"

Fuck. Haven's eyes are cartoon wide. My belly twists on itself; it could be the eggnog, but it feels a lot like…shame. It's weird. My hatred of Christmas is legit, even though I don't tell anyone why, because I never care what people think. It's no one's business, but the look on her face is similar to the look Hendricks, Miles, and Clemmie always give me.

"And I thought you only hated Slipknot," Haven mutters from the corner of her mouth, only audible to me, and I decide that maybe I don't hate Slipknot after all, because they gave me the best opener with this insanely hot girl.

"Hey, look at all these decorations…" says Hendricks, thankfully changing the subject.

The three of us stand there, taking in the store and its Aladdin's Cave–esque quality; drawers full of brightly colored baubles and ribbons, wreaths, paper chains, knitted stockings, snow globes, nutcracker statues, glittery objects, stars—a plethora of Christmas paraphernalia. It's everywhere.

Wylder Trees is not just a tree shop. It's a *Christmas* shop. This girl, Haven, *loves* Christmas.

"Wow, it's amazing," I say, truthfully, because it is. There doesn't seem to be a surface un-Christmassed. It's just not my taste, though thankfully I've not broken out in hives.

Because *that's* happened.

"Yeah, I love it here," she replies with a smile that hits right in the center of my chest. "And that's the greatest compliment from a Christmas hater."

I don't correct her, I'm too preoccupied watching Miles try not to laugh, and when

Haven turns to help Hendricks, Miles mouths *Grinch.*

Yeah, he's definitely getting disowned, but before I can tell him, he runs off again to wait with Lando, who's guarding our tree from any prospective other buyers. They each take hold of one end and guide it onto the street.

I stay where I am—too scared to touch anything—and wait until Haven and Hendricks come back to the till, both their arms laden with decorations. Everything's dumped on the counter. From the looks of it, this is all to take back to Max, his son.

"You know"—he points to the giant nutcracker statues—"I'll take them, too, but can you deliver the tree, and then we can take these back in the car?"

She nods. "Of course. I can have the statues shipped express to England if it's easier for you, we can get them there before Christmas."

"Oh no, that's fine, thank you. We can manage," he replies, because they'll come on the plane home with us. "Just getting the tree to the cabin is all we need."

"You got it." She picks up a large pair of scissors, scoring it through a huge roll of Bubble Wrap, which is when I notice her fingernails.

Alternate red and green with tiny drawings of Santa and candy canes, and *all things Christmas*. Before I can stop myself, the image of her lips around my cock is replaced by those Christmas nails.

"So are you boys tree decorating today? Or hitting the slopes?"

I stare at her mouth. I *know* she just said something, but for the life of me, I didn't hear it because my mind is elsewhere. Somewhere *way* south of the gutter.

"Al…" The confusion on Hendricks's face is valid. I'm confused too. Jolted, even. "Haven asked what we were doing today."

"Oh. Sorry. Slopes first, then the tree this afternoon. I need to shake off this hangover."

Haven giggles. "Go to Aspen Mountain. After yesterday's blizzard, the snow will be amazing."

"How often do you go up there?"

"As often as I can, but I haven't been for a couple weeks." She gently places the first few things she's wrapped for Hendricks into a large store bag and smiles at him. "You picked some really cute ornaments. Some of my favorites."

I decide to leave them to it and wander around the store myself. It is pretty cool, I can't deny it. Our mother would buy out the whole place if she were here. *It's the sort of shop we should have in Valentine Nook,* I think, while also keeping one eye trained on Haven and the way she's laughing at Hendricks.

I pick up a bauble to distract myself. I don't want to see Haven laughing with anyone else. I want all her laughs.

By the time she's done wrapping up Hendricks's stuff, I've picked up so many distraction baubles that I need both hands to hold them. I'm also not quite sure where I got them from.

"Al…what're you doing?"

Haven peers at my full hands. "Did you want me to wrap them?"

"Um…" My eyes flick to Hendricks, whose brow is quirked. "Yeah. Yes. I'll take them home for Mum and Clemmie. That's my sister," I add quickly, *and totally unnecessarily*.

"Cool. That's nice of you."

"And you know what…I'll take that too." I point to a star sitting on a shelf. It's the biggest, most glittery and opulent one I can find, and it costs four hundred dollars. Fuck Christmas. "It can go on Miles's bloody tree."

Hendricks says nothing. He doesn't need to, he's trying too hard not to laugh.

"You got it, *Grinch*." Haven winks.

Why does it sound different when she says it?

merry
christmas

Haven

5

I'm staring down at the broken remains of the seven hundred thousandth gingerbread house I've knocked off the prep counter.

I wish I'd never volunteered to help with this stupid competition. Or come up with the idea in the first place.

"Oh, goddamn it," I hiss under my breath, but everyone is far too busy to hear me, and no one even so much as glances up from whatever mixing bowl they're in charge of today.

I'm very tempted to kick it under the counter. It would be

so easy. But I'd only have to deal with it later when Kyle, the head baker, notices. He got annoyed when I broke the first one. He was *super* annoyed when I broke the tenth one. It's anyone's guess what will happen if he sees this.

At this point I don't know why he's not moved them someplace safer. At least this batch will be sold and out of here by lunchtime.

Saylor's head pops around the door frame just as I'm resting mine against the wall, because honestly, I. Am. Exhausted.

"You want a coffee?"

I crack one eye. "It's like you're inside my brain."

"Ew." Her face screws up in disgust, which, quite frankly, I take offense to because my brain is a delight to be inside of most of the time. *Some* of the time.

"Yes, I want a coffee." I push off the wall and grab the broom, quickly disposing of the evidence.

"Really you should be making me one, ya know," she mutters as we walk onto the bakery floor.

"Yeah, how'd you figure that one?"

"I'd still be in bed if it weren't for you."

I have no response. The girl ain't lying.

Here's the problem. Both of us are suckers.

This bakery, in which the pair of us are currently standing at 6:05 a.m., belongs to Mrs. Loughty, a seventy-two-year-old Aspen native. She set the bakery up thirty years ago, and it's been a flagship of the community ever since. Her cinnamon buns, I swear to god, people have murdered over them—well, committed a low-grade felony, but that's another story.

The bakery grew over the years and started serving drinks. Now by six thirty every morning, there's a fully formed line around the block for the first hot chocolates and buns of the day to take up the mountain. In the summer, it's strawberry iced tea.

Tourists come for the canvas store bags, which became a coveted item after *Vogue* featured them a few years ago in a round-up of the best local Aspen hot spots.

Anyway, I digress.

Sadly, Mrs. Loughty's husband, Chip, died at the end of last year, and since the two of them never had kids, she's found herself with a lot more time on her hands. I always liked the Loughtys; Chip worked with my dad a little, and when Saylor and I were younger, Mrs. L would let us pick out one thing from behind the counter every time we came in for a fresh loaf of bread. I *always* picked a cinnamon bun.

Therefore, when he died, I said I would help her with anything she wanted. She just had to let me know.

In October, she cashed my promise in *big time* and asked me to help out during the holidays.

Of course, I had said. *And Saylor's around to help too. Whatever you need, Mrs. Loughty.*

Six weeks ago, she handed us the keys and promptly took off on a three-month round-the-world cruise with her sister. She didn't want to spend Christmas in Aspen without Chip.

Five weeks ago, I was reminded about the annual gingerbread competition, which the bakery runs every year. An idea *I'd* come up with as a teenager.

If time travel were a thing, I'd go back and tape my mouth shut.

The only saving grace about this entire situation is the team of bakers who come in on rotation starting at four a.m. No way I could bake two thousand gingerbread kits. Saylor and I only have the admin to deal with.

Oh, and all the customers who want the early morning hot chocolates.

Thankfully the place closes at lunchtime. It's probably why there's always such a rush in the mornings, but no matter how many times she's been begged to keep the bakery open for longer, the hours have always remained the same. Seven a.m. to twelve p.m.

I've gotten through the last month by choosing to believe Mrs. Loughty forgot I also have my own store to run. On the flip side, I really need the money. I'm not sure how Saylor's dealt with the early mornings—mostly on coffee and cinnamon buns I think. Plus, she gets to nap in the afternoon once she's closed the store.

Me, I leave here at nine a.m. to go and open the tree shop, then come back here to straighten up after the baking crew is done at five p.m.

Saylor hands me a steaming cup of coffee I willingly admit is the best coffee in Colorado. Maybe the United States. Everything about this store is amazing. When you don't have to open up at the ass crack of dawn, that is.

"Thanks." I lift my cup to knock against hers. "I need this."

She groans so loudly I'm tempted to add another shot of caffeine to her cup. "Excited for the competition?"

I shrug, but I can't hold back the smile that breaks the solemn line of my mouth.

Christmas is my favorite time of year. Period.

There's nothing about it I don't love. The cold,

the constant scent of cinnamon and spice in the air, the twinkle and glitter, carols…all of it.

My parents loved it, and every year grew more and more excited as the year came to a close. My mom would start hanging winter decorations on November 1, replacing the ones she'd put up for Halloween. Once Thanksgiving was over, the real Christmassy ones would come out. We're talking life-sized Santa and a full sleigh in the driveway, nutcrackers flanking the front porch, and twinkle lights on every tree around the house to shine through the snowy branches.

When I was little, we would always decorate a gingerbread house, which is where the gingerbread competition came in. So, yeah, this is the week I look forward to most in December.

"Of course I am. It's the *gingerbread house competition*. But…" I hold a finger in the air and pout. "I'm bummed we can't take part."

"We should sneak one in." Saylor grins,

because this year will be the first year we won't have entered, because we're running it instead. "We can come up with a fake name."

I lift an eyebrow. I'm tempted. Very tempted.

I'm trying not to think about it.

The competition runs for three days, and during that time, it's the most talked about event in Aspen. The rules are simple:

1. *Collect your gingerbread house frame and icing tubes from the bakery for $50 (proceeds to the local charity)*

2. *Bring back a fully decorated house by the end of the week.**

3. *Judges decision is final*

**Entries can only include regular baking or household products that are readily available to be bought from a store.*

Mrs. Loughty had to add that last point when the competition started to get out of hand.

One year, a couple of dads had a game of one-upmanship for their daughters to win the gingerbread house trophy. What had begun as a day on the mountains turned into a competition of who attended the best school, drove the newest car, had the most ponies, and descended into outright warfare when one of the girls declared she was going to win the gingerbread prize, and the rest of them started crying.

One dad rolled up several thousand-dollar bills into the dough to use as drainpipes around the house and told Mrs. L she could keep it. Another dropped by the store after hours and not-so-subtly offered his Caribbean island to her for vacation, while a third said she could use his plane.

It all went in the charity box.

Part of me wonders if Mrs. Loughty knew exactly what she was doing when she left before the holiday rush.

I'm about to reply to Saylor when the scent of a new batch of hot cinnamon buns hits me, and Brock, one of the bakers, appears from the kitchen looking flustered. "Kyle says five minutes to opening. And he knows you broke another house, Haven."

My eyes practically roll to the heavens. I take the tray he's holding and slide it into place on the counter pain, giving one last glance around. Everything is ready.

Pastry boxes are stacked and waiting to be filled. Beans are ground. Croissants, plain and flavored, sit next to the cinnamon buns, English scones, brownies, meringues, and assorted other pastries. On the next row of trays sits decorated Christmas gingerbread—reindeer, Santas, candy canes, stockings…five different types of bread are neatly stacked on the shelves behind us.

Most importantly, the first set of canvas bags containing the gingerbread house building kit—four walls and the roof, plus all the icing—are all stored on the center table, set around a beautifully festive, finished, and extra Christmassy house Kyle made yesterday.

Saylor eyes the long line outside and snatches up the store keys, twirling the keyring around her index finger. "Okay. I'm opening."

It only takes ten minutes before the trays are being refilled.

Between us, Saylor and I almost holler ourselves hoarse as we let the guys in the kitchen know the bread, buns, croissants, cookies, or gingerbread are nearly out. Brock comes out with a third batch of cinnamon buns, and it's so busy that Saylor refuses to let him go, so he's now making the drinks while she packs the boxes.

Forty-five minutes in, and there's finally a lull as the end of the line is reached, even though it's still busy. Brock gets called back to the mixing bowls, but only until we need him again. Half the gingerbread houses have been sold, and I'm tidying up the table when a deep voice injects me with so much energy it feels like I've got a sugar rush.

I spin around and come face to face with Alex, The Christmas Hater, and his very wide chest.

It must be the tiredness I feel acutely in the back of my brain that caused me to forget about this insanely hot guy, with the sexiest accent I've ever heard. Like Theo James soaked himself in a vat of honey. Is it possible to be turned on by an accent?

And the way he smells…maybe I didn't notice yesterday because the smell of pine in my shop is so overpowering, but here, among the sugar and spice, *he's* the *all things nice.* A delicious, earthy scent, like leather and ivy, evoking cozy nights camping under the stars.

I'm fighting a desperate urge to lick him, which I hope is because I've been living solely on gingerbread and need to refresh my palate.

Why is every cell in my body throbbing?

"I thought it was you." He grins, and I find

myself stuck in that same spell as yesterday. The one that stopped me from looking away from him. Because all I can do is stare into his deep blue eyes. "Don't tell me you own this place too? In fact, is this town just run by one person? Are *you* Aspen?"

A laugh escapes me. "No, sadly. I'm just regular Haven."

"I don't think there's anything regular about you?" he replies without any hesitation, and the way he holds my gaze makes me feel like I've stepped into one of Kyle's ovens. Naked.

I'm feverishly hot.

Was that coffee double strength? There's no way my heart would be pounding this hard otherwise, that would account for the weird sugar rush too.

Is he ever going to look away?

"Um…well, I am, and, uh…no." I scratch my head, trying to remember what he just asked. "I'm just helping out a friend for the season."

His smile widens. "That's very kind of you."

"Aren't you going heli-skiing today?" I blurt.

"Yes, we are. But I volunteered to come down to the bakery—*this bakery*—we saw yesterday and pick up whatever you're selling." His gaze slowly roams around the shop floor. "I can understand why there was such a huge queue."

"Yeah, it's only open in the mornings, so everyone comes early before it runs out. You got here just in time."

"Thank goodness." He grins, his focus finding me again, and I forget what I was going to say.

"Hey, Al…" One of the twins steps in next to Alex. "What are we buying? This place is bloody packed. I'm getting in the line, otherwise we'll be here forever."

"Hendricks,"—Alex nudges his brother and nods toward me—"remember Haven?"

Hendricks's double take is just like the one I gave him and his twin. Guess he wasn't expecting to see me here either. His eyes flick from me back to Alex, his grin widening, and I feel like I'm on the outside of a joke. "Of course…Haven. How could I forget the Christmas tree lady?"

I curtsey, and immediately wish I hadn't because *what the fuck…*

I've never curtsied in my life. I only know how to do it because I've seen it on *Bridgerton*. And *Downton Abbey*. It *has* to be that accent.

"The very one," I finally answer.

But Hendricks's attention is now on the table. "Huh, that's cool. Al…check out the gingerbread house."

"Yeah, Hen. It's cool," Alex replies, but barely looks at it because he's too busy looking at me.

Which is flattering and all, but *not this week.*

Not *gingerbread house* week. He might be a Christmas hater but he's going to have to take that Grinch energy somewhere else.

"Kyle, our head baker, made it. The competition opened today."

"Competition?"

"Yep, the gingerbread house competition. It's all anyone will talk about for the next three days. It's for real Christmas *lovers*." I grin wide. "Not for Grinches."

Hendricks barks a laugh, and slaps Alex on the back. "She got you there, Al."

"It's a big, *big* deal. Lots of pressure."

But then their expressions change from amusement to skepticism. Doesn't stop them from being less extraordinarily good looking though. Not at all.

"Pressure? For gingerbread?" Alex smirks, his blue eyes glittering in amusement and those dimples of his are on full display. My body heats up another degree. Tiny pulses clench in my core when he curls his fingers in a *gimme* gesture, because I'm imagining him doing it in a very different scenario. "Okay, tree lady, give me the sales pitch."

"There's no pitch." I pick up one of the competition fliers I was straightening and hand it over. "You buy one of the house kits. You have the next three days to assemble it and drop it back here with your name badge attached. Each house is judged, and the winners are announced on Saturday morning."

Hendricks leans into Alex, both of them reading the rules. "What do we win?"

"The honor of winning, plus a trophy."

Hendricks barks another laugh, while Alex's smile broadens.

Crossing my arms, I take a step back and throw him my own humoring smirk. "About two thousand people will enter."

Hendricks's air of indifference drops. "What?! Two thousand? That's more than the whole of Valentine Nook."

I don't know what that means, but I give the pair of them my most smug expression, anyway. "Hey, we're a competitive bunch in Aspen. Winning the title of Best Gingerbread House means something."

I can tell from the look on both their faces

they don't believe me. Though I forget all about the gingerbread house when Alex sucks in his plump lower lip, adding a head tilt.

I need to schedule an early night with my vibrator, stat.

"Okay. You're on. I'll take four kits."

Hendricks scoffs. "Al, seriously, c'mon—"

"Hey, you and Miles aren't the only ones who can plan fun. I'm buying them, and *we're* doing it. You made me decorate the stupid…" His eyes slice to mine, and back to Hendricks. "Um, I mean…you made me decorate the tree yesterday, *you're* doing *this*."

This time Hendricks stays silent. His eyes are doing all the talking as they flick between Alex and me; 50 percent confused, 50 percent amused, and I've no doubt it's the exact same look Saylor is giving me.

I can feel it from where she's standing behind the counter, because miraculously the store is now empty, so she's got nothing to do except watch this entire interaction.

I turn around, and yup, I'm correct. She's even got one eyebrow raised.

Alex gathers up four gingerbread house kits and drops them into Hendricks's arms. "That's that, now what else do we have to buy in here?"

He sweeps a discerning eye around the room, over every stacked table, shelf, and finally, a fully replenished counter, before landing back on me expectantly.

"What do you like?"

"Anything and everything. We walked past yesterday, and it looked fun." He grins at me. Hendricks drops his head with a subtle shake. Not *that* subtle though. "I have three hungry brothers to feed."

I guide the pair of them over to my favorite part of the store, the counter. "Okay, you need to try our cinnamon buns. They're what people come for the most. Plus, the hot chocolate."

"Okay, four of each. What else?"

"Um…" I start, my mouth filling with cotton wool and I completely blank on what we sell, even as I'm looking at it. But there's something about this guy that's made me lose all my words this morning.

"Our sourdough is awesome. The chocolate croissants are fresh from the oven, and we have Christmas cookies, and some authentic English scones. You folks are English, right? You can give us your verdict," Saylor interrupts.

"Excellent. We'll take four of everything."

Behind Alex, Hendricks is openly laughing though he doesn't seem to notice, and his broad smile never drops as Saylor and I pack the boxes and boxes of everything they've bought, and ring up the total.

"Hang on." Hendricks looks at me as I scan in the final gingerbread kit. "How long do these things keep for?"

"You have to bring it back by Thursday."

"But they won't go stale if I take one back to England?"

"Um…no. It'll be fine. You want to make it at home?"

"I'll make it with my son."

"You have a son?" I blurt before I can stop myself, because even I can hear it's a weird question. Why couldn't he have a son?

Nothing to do with the fact it's automatically made me wonder if Alex has a son too. And if he's even single. And why am I thinking about him naked?

Shut up, Haven.

But Hendricks doesn't notice if it's weird. In fact, his face lights up with so much love it punches me right in the chest.

"I do, he's three."

"Tell you what…" Rushing to pick up a fifth kit, before I make things more weird, I place it in the tote bag on top of the rest. "I'll throw it in for free, seeing as you're not entering, and you've bought half the store."

"That's very kind, thank you." He smiles. Interestingly, this smile does nothing for me.

No, the core-clenching, butterfly-fluttering feeling I get seems to be solely reserved for Alex's.

"You're welcome."

"Hendricks is the only one of us responsible enough to have a kid," Alex adds, except the way he says it makes me wonder if he just read my mind and he's trying to tell me he's single, especially when he adds, "Are you going to meet me at the jukebox later? I need that code to save me from the Christmas music."

As I pass him the final store bag, his thumb brushes over mine and my entire body zings with electricity.

"Maybe."

"Then *maybe* I'll see you later. If not, I'll be back to drop off my house."

"I saw those guys in the bar the other night," hisses Saylor right in my ear as Alex and Hendricks step to one side and let another group of customers in before they leave. "They're super hot."

"Uh-hmm."

"And the one with the stubble is definitely into you," she continues. "And you know what?"

"What?"

"You're into him too. You should totally hook up with him."

Saylor dodges the elbow I try to jab her with and goes back to stocking the shelves. Except she's singing *Haven's gonna have sex* while she does.

It's not the worst idea.

Merry
Christmas

Alexander

6

"Al's got the hots for the Christmas tree lady."

The statement cuts through the deafening whirr of the rotor blades, ringing out loud and clear in my headset. My head flicks to Hendricks, and I shoot him my best daggered glare, which only makes him laugh.

Sometimes it's hard to tell who's the bigger shit stirrer. Him or Miles. At least with Miles you expect it. Hendricks is like a silent assassin, striking when you're weak.

Little shit.

"I have not."

"Yeah, then why are we decorating gingerbread houses? And why did you spend five hundred dollars on muffins."

"It wasn't five hundred dollars. And it wasn't muffins."

It *wasn't*. Not quite, it was four hundred. And if you take into account that everything in Aspen is ten times more expensive than anywhere else, it reduces the overall cost to approximately twenty-five dollars. Which is a perfectly reasonable amount to spend on bread, cinnamon rolls, and gingerbread. Not a bloody muffin in sight.

I'd spend ten times that if I got to see her blush again because that shade of pink on her cheeks did something to me. Yeah. Five thousand dollars on cinnamon buns would be a bargain.

"Who've you got the hots for?" shouts Lando, which is the first full sentence he's uttered all morning.

"No one," I reply at the same time Hendricks,

the rat, repeats, "The Christmas tree lady."

"Haven?" asks Miles.

"Yup."

"Yeah, we already know. It was totally obvious yesterday. I was expecting to come down and see her at breakfast with us." Miles's brows waggle.

I roll my eyes. It's pointless denying it, because yeah, she's super hot. I turn my attention back to the view outside; we're soaring over Aspen Mountain, everything below is the perfect blanket of pristine white snow. In the distance, the gondolas are transporting today's skiers to the top for them to zoom back down to the bottom, and repeat.

Being outside, breathing in the clean, fresh, freezing air, it's about as far away from London as you can get. Which reminds me why we're here. To distract Lando from what's going on back home, to take his mind off what we'll be returning to, and to give him a break. It's time for the four of us to be together as brothers because we haven't done it since Lando met Caroline.

It's not so I can shag the first girl I meet.

Plus, if anyone's going to behave like that, it's Miles.

Pulling my phone out to snap a picture of the ground whizzing past us, a message pops up. I groan as I realize it's not just one, but an entire thread.

Burlington Fam Chat

Miles the Great:
Hey, Clem. Al's got the hots for a girl.

Clemmie: What? Who?

Miles the Great: Guess.

Clemmie:
Milo, how am I supposed to guess?

Henners: *eye roll emoji*

Henners:
It's the local Christmas tree seller.

Clemmie:
Christmas tree? Al, are you feeling okay?

Miles the Great:
He's actually looking a little flushed right now. He's been blushing A LOT since we got here *blushing face emoji*

Alex:
I'm sitting across from you, dickhead. You're going to be flushed in a minute when I throttle you.

Miles the Great:
Spoken like someone harboring a true crush.

Clemmie:
Never thought I'd see the day Alex fancied someone who likes Christmas.

Lando:
She doesn't like Christmas. She luuurves it. And we're all making gingerbread houses tomorrow because she sold them to him.

Henners:
He bought half her Christmas shop yesterday. He's changing.

Clemmie:
speechless emoji
heart eyes emoji
kissy face emoji

Clemmie:
Does this mean you'll come for Christmas morning and we can do stockings this year?

Clemmie:
Wait. Oh my god. Wait!

Clemmie:
Are you filling her stocking?

Next to me, Miles snorts so loudly and quickly he starts choking, which descends into a full-on coughing fit. I don't bother slapping him on the back, though maybe I should.

Alex:
Why do I have the most annoying family?

Clemmie:
Love you too, Al.

Clemmie:
How're you doing, Lanny?

There's silence—as silent as you can be in a helicopter. Miles holds in another cough as we wait for Lando to respond, because though we've all been together the past few days, he's barely spoken.

Lando: Fine.

With that, Lando shuts his phone off. Miles is still typing away, but I shut mine off, too, just to stop the incessant buzzing of messages.

In my periphery, I see Miles's mouth open, no doubt ready to throw out another deluge of annoying comments about me having the hots for Haven. Like he's got nothing else to talk about.

"This week isn't about girls," I snap loudly, before covering the microphone of my headset and jerking my head in Lando's direction so Miles knows *exactly* what I'm talking about. "It's about taking *his* mind off things."

"Hey," Lando grumbles from the seat behind, because I'm obviously not that subtle, and he's not blind, and I was speaking into a microphone. "Don't bring me into this. I don't care what you do."

I shake my head, even more so when Miles adds, "For your information, I was about to say we're nearly at the first drop-off. And I don't care what you do, either, Al. Though if you ask me, getting laid might cheer you up a bit. So maybe you should try it. Been quite a while, hasn't it?"

Hendricks laughs loudly.

"I don't need to get laid." I grit out, turning back to the windows.

I *do* need to get laid.

But it's not been *quite a while*—it's been a couple of months at most—though that's likely a death sentence in Miles's world. But I broke up with my ex-girlfriend because she wanted to *take the next step in our relationship* and I did *not*.

I'm still contemplating my lack of sex life and trying harder not to think about having sex with Haven, when I realize we're descending. Five minutes later, the doors of the helicopter slide open, and we breathe in that perfect mountain air I was talking about. There's a second of silence as we take it all in, but only a second because then the guide is running through safety checks, including avalanche warning signs and directions for the pickup location.

He's barely finished before the least responsible, but annoyingly and arguably better skier—not that I'd ever admit it out loud—has pulled on his helmet, clipped in, and taken off.

"Race you to the bottom. Last one there needs to get laid." Miles's voice echoes around the mountain.

It's followed by, "Miles, you shit," as Lando, Hendricks, and I all flick down our visors and chase after him.

My stance on not needing to get laid lasts all day.

It's there through the first mountain drop, a long lunch followed by two more mountain drops, a change of clothes, an argument about whether to go to The Little Nell or The Old Saloon for drinks, and up to the point where we walk through the doors of The Old Saloon. I barely notice the live band playing Christmas music because Haven is the first person I see.

She's standing behind the bar, her hair's piled on top of her head, and she's all flustered, pouring out a beer from the tap. Her lower lip juts out as she tries and fails to blow a lone tendril of hair away from her eyes. There's a giant ball of mistletoe hanging almost directly above her, and all I can think about is kissing her.

Big deal, I want to kiss her.

It's certainly not why I'm walking over to stand in front of her while ordering my brothers to find the nearest available table next to the fire, and telling them I'll get the drinks.

"Need a hand?" I ask.

Her green eyes shoot up and widen. "Oh, hey, Alex. Hey…um, how's it goin'?"

"Great." I grin, while she puffs again at the blonde strand stuck to her long, thick eyelashes. It's making her look like she has some kind of twitch. "May I?"

I reach out as she blinks again, carefully remove the errant hair, and tuck it behind her ear.

"Oh, thank you." She smiles wide, her eyelashes fluttering free this time as a pink hue creeps up her cheeks. She places the beer glass down on the tray and picks up an empty one. It's then I realize that she's on the wrong side of the bar.

I'm fairly certain they don't allow patrons to pour their own beers, therefore I've found another place she's working at.

"You know, I'm starting to believe that you run the town." I laugh. "Are you the mayor?"

She groans, and I feel that groan right in my dick.

"I wish. If I were the mayor, I'd give myself

the day off."

"When *do* you have a day off?"

"Um..." She looks at her watch. "Today's Monday, so that would make it the day after never."

"What?" I laugh, though I'm slightly aghast. "You must have a day off."

Another empty glass is picked up to fill. "We're short-staffed tonight, so I'm helping out."

"But you must have a day off, surely?" I press, because if she doesn't have a day off, how am I supposed to see her socially and create an opportunity that will lead to us having sex?

Hypothetically.

I never get her response, however, as a guy I recognize from the other night comes up to the bar and drops his tray on the counter with a loud clatter. "Two bottles of Bollinger, four of the Snowmass IPAs, and four eggnogs."

An involuntary wretch squeezes my

throat at the idea of drinking eggnog again. "That stuff needs to come with a warning."

"Hey, it's our best seller." He chuckles, though only halfheartedly, and as I turn to peer at him, I notice his face has taken on a greenish tinge.

Maybe he's had too many eggnogs.

Before I can ask him, he takes off with the beers Haven has finished pouring, and I lurch forward from a heavy clap on my back.

"Al…what are you—" Lando starts, then spots Haven, who's pouring out a jar of spicy crackers. "Oh, never mind."

Haven's eyes snap up. "Hey, there. Lando, right?"

"One and the same." He salutes her. Dipping his mouth closer to my ear so only I can hear, he says, "You need to wipe the drool off your chin, brother."

My hand's already swiping at my mouth before I realize he's got me. "Idiot."

"Come on." He tugs at my arm and throws his around my shoulder. "Try to play a little hard to get. You took too long. Miles ordered food and drinks. And found a deck of cards."

A deck of cards only means one thing.

"We're playing snap."

My eyes widen. "In public?"

"Yeah, it'll be fine. C'mon."

Turning my attention back to Haven—not that it really left—I thumb behind me. "I'll be over with the boys, think you could ask the band to play something more Slipknot-y?"

I'm rewarded with a hefty eye roll and a rumble of laughter, before she nods her head. "I'll see what I can do."

"Thanks." I throw her a grin and follow Lando to the table, where an ice-cold beer is waiting for me.

We're going to need Slipknot to drown out the noise—though, this Christmas band seems to be doing its best to deafen people. Burlington snap can get…*animated*…because when you have four guys all wanting to slam the table at the same time, it's noisy and can lead to an expensive repair bill.

Hendricks looks up from shuffling cards quicker than a Vegas pro. "Something more interesting over at the bar, Alexander?"

"Much more interesting." I drop into the empty seat next to him, which also happens to be next to the fire, and remove my coat and sweater before I die of heat exhaustion. "What's the dare?"

Ever since we were kids, the four of us, plus Clemmie when we allowed her to, played snap. Instead of playing for money—because none of us had any at ten years old—each round counted toward a point, and the player with the least points at the end of the game had to perform a dare.

They started out small (ish), like the time Lando dared me to steal some food coloring from the Burlington kitchens and dye our family golden retriever pink. Or when Hendricks switched out all the sugar for salt. But as we got older they became a little more extreme. Once, Hendricks had to pretend he was Miles on a date with Miles's new girlfriend, who couldn't tell the difference between them. But he wasn't allowed to make out with her, and spent the whole afternoon dodging her mouth.

"Loser has to pick up a girl." Miles grins, looking directly at Lando.

Lando seems to have a different opinion, given he's now wiping droplets of spluttered beer off his chin. "I never agreed to that."

"Too bad, not up to you to decide. I lost the last game, therefore I get to name the dare."

"I'm not picking up a girl."

I scoop up a handful of the spicy crackers that had been left with our beer, throw them in my mouth, and lean back in my chair, trying my hardest not to laugh. "If you lose, you have to. You know the rules, Lan."

"There are loads of really hot girls in here. It's not going to be hard," offers Hendricks, slightly more conciliatorily, but there's no hiding the grin he's not bothering to hold in. "We're playing until the food arrives. Loser will be announced then."

All four of us look around, and it's true there are a lot of *really* hot girls in here, including a big group who've just arrived, dressed like they're on a bachelorette party. But my eyes land back on tonight's barmaid. She's easily the hottest girl in here, and the only one I have any desire to look at.

The thought briefly occurs to me to throw the game and lose so I have an excuse to kiss her. She might not have been a breakfast guest this morning, but we've got a few mornings left here to accomplish that.

"Fine." Lando huffs, and his eyes narrow at Miles.

"So you agree to the dare?" he replies, and holds his hand out.

"Yup. I'll find a girl. But that's only if I lose, and I *never* lose." A pointed smile crooks Lando's lip, and he places his palm on the back of Miles's hand. Hendricks and I follow.

The dare has been sealed and agreed to.

Miles pins Lando with a look of his own. A look I know well, and it's usually followed by a whole lot of trouble. "We'll see. Deal the cards, Henners."

Hendricks flicks each card around the table until we have a neat pile in front of us. "As the previous loser, Milo goes first."

Miles takes his time, sipping his beer as slowly as possible, which Lando refuses to rise to. He just sits there patiently waiting for Miles to peel a card off the top of his stack and place it down, which he does. His palm barely lifts from the table, however; something Lando's not quite so patient about.

"Milo, lift your hand," he orders. "Six inches off the table. And that's most definitely not six inches."

"That's what she said." Miles snorts, but raises his hand a little higher.

Lando places his card—an ace of hearts—on top of Miles's, but a flinch of his hand has Miles slamming his palm on the table loud enough for the group next to us to turn around.

"Rookie mistake, little brother." Lando smirks. "And that's minus one to you."

Oh, I forgot to mention, the trick to Burlington snap was to fake your turn enough that your opponent slammed first, but not at the expense of an actual snap of the cards. Which is exactly why it can get rowdy.

Miles throws a cracker into his mouth. "Don't worry, just lulling you into a false sense of security."

"Yeah, yeah."

Hendricks places next, and I follow. We manage to get through another rotation of the table without anyone slamming their hand, and more importantly, breaking anything. The following rounds, we aren't so lucky when Miles, in his enthusiasm, sends the bowl of chili crackers flying, and only Lando's lightning reflexes—as he grabs it midair—stops it from smacking the guy behind us in the head.

I refrain from once more pointing out that Burlington snap should never be played in public, because Lando is now laughing so hard I almost forget why we're here in Aspen, at Christmas, because I'm trying to remember the last time I saw him laugh like that. But I can't.

And as annoying as Miles is, his best quality is making people laugh.

"Ooh, food is here. Game is over," Miles cries, just as a tray of huge burgers and fries is placed in front of us. "Tally on the points?"

Hendricks stuffs a fry into his mouth and looks down at his phone, where he's been keeping track. "Miles two, Lando zero, Al and me one point."

"How the fuck am I zero?" snaps Lando. "I won the last round."

"Yeah, but twice you slammed early," Hendricks replies, so straight-faced I realize the twins have set up this entire game just so Lando loses.

Just so Lando has fun and forgets everything waiting back home in England. At least for one more day. *For Lando.*

"No way! Al lost more than I did."

"I did not," I protest, and peer over to Haven again. I wouldn't mind losing so much…

The sound of glasses breaking has everyone turning around to the end of the bar, where the guy from earlier slumps against it. Haven rushes to his side, along with another person, the older guy Haven pointed out the other night, I assume must be the owner—and they help him to his feet. I'm waiting for someone to ask for a doctor, but a third person steps in who seems to have assumed the role.

A couple of minutes later and everyone's lost interest. Drinks are being drunk, the boys are eating like they've forgotten how to chew, and the band is back to playing annoying-as-hell Christmas music. But as the doors fling open again, and another crowd of après-skiers enters, I catch the look on Haven's face.

She already said they were short-staffed tonight, and now they're down by two more, because the older guy and the one who collapsed have left with the doctor.

Before I can think any more about it, I finish my burger, stand up, and walk over to the bar.

Merry Christmas

Haven

7

Ever since Alex walked in with his brothers, it's like he's had a spotlight on him, or a magnet, tractor beam maybe, because something's made sure that *no matter what,* I know where he is and what he's doing.

Which right now, is walking over to me.

It's *super* annoying.

Tonight's busy enough without me being distracted to the point of knocking over drinks or pouring beer until the glass is overflowing, because I haven't been paying attention. So far tonight, my entire focus is on Alex and his supreme English hotness. I didn't even know they made them like that in England.

But they do. Alex is proof. His brothers are backup proof. Seriously, they're all hot.

There must be *some* genes in that family.

I could be out there, flirting, collecting glasses or whatever, but I may as well be surgically attached to this beer tap for all I've moved.

Mike had to choose tonight of all nights to catch the flu (eye roll) and knock himself out when he fell over. Sorry, that sounds unsupportive. But *you know*…and then Joe had to go with him to the hospital, so we're down much-needed staff.

Boone and Jocelyn, working at the other end of the bar, haven't moved either. They've spent all night pouring shots and opening bottles of champagne. There are three of us working a six-man bar.

Soon patrons are going to start getting annoyed at how slow the service is. They might seem chill right now, but it turns on a dime when they're thirsty and left waiting. I've seen it happen.

Alex is now ten yards away. Unlike this

morning, he's not wearing a beanie. His thick, brown curls brush along the collar of his shirt, while the rest is swept away from his face in that really annoying boy way that stays put forever, unlike mine, which gets everywhere. I watch him sidestep a couple of girls charging over to the dance floor when the band starts a country version of "Jingle Bells," and he rolls his eyes.

But as he nears the spot at the bar where I'm standing, he walks straight past. The disappointment sinking in my belly only lasts a couple of seconds when he ducks under the bar hatch.

"Wh-what are you doing?" I shout to him over a particularly loud guitar riff.

"Helping."

"What?"

"I'm helping you. You need help, right? It's *busy*." His eyes sweep around the bar in case I didn't realize.

I glance over to Boone and Jocelyn to see

what they think, but neither notice we now have an extra pair of hands, so I'm making the executive decision. Plus, this is how I usually find myself working behind the bar, because Joe never seems to hire enough staff per night, and I'm regularly drafted in when I only came for a quiet drink.

"Yeah, we're busy. Sure…thank you. But…um…do you know what to do?"

He doesn't look like the kind of guy who's spent any time serving drinks. He looks like the kind of guy who gets served them.

The kind of guy who belongs in Aspen.

The kind of guy who drops four hundred bucks on cinnamon buns. And a thousand on Christmas tree decorations.

"I worked for two summers in The Cupid's Arrow," he yells back.

"What?" I don't know what the hell that means, which he can clearly tell from the way my face is screwed up.

"Never mind. Yes, I know what to do." He picks up an empty glass and starts pouring perfectly.

I place a full beer on the tray, ready for collection, and shift closer to Alex.

"Okay, this is how it works. One of the floor team will drop their order tab on the bar in front of you, along with a tray. Glasses are behind you. All the beers are on tap, the champagne is in the fridges, the liquor's on the shelf, organized by color, and the eggnog is in the urn. We're not fancy in here, we like to keep it simple."

That grin of his breaks across his face, and when he winks, heat pools in my cheeks *and* in my core.

"Got it. Nothing fancy. Glasses, beer, shots, fizz." His blue eyes twinkle mischievously as he leans in closer; it's enough that the scent of him—delicate musky oak—hits me right between my thighs. "But I'm not going near that eggnog."

My face splits with a laugh—the perfect release to cut through whatever this thing is building between us—and I slide back into position at my beer tap. My eyes automatically land on the spot near the fire where Alex's brothers are watching him. There's no disguising the identical expressions of amusement on all their faces. Even the older one with the thick, dark stubble has cracked a smile. It's nice. Not as nice as the guy standing to my left opening champagne like a professional, but nice.

Jack, one of the floor team, drops his tray on the bar in front of me.

"Who's the new guy?"

"A friend, helping out while Mike is sick."

"Wasn't he sitting at that table by the fire?"

"Yeah, and now he's helping because it's hella busy in here."

"Cool cool. Got that right," he shouts behind him, disappearing into the crowds with a full tray of drinks lifted above his head.

At least we're too busy for anyone to ask too many questions.

One of the kitchen staff brings over a full

rack of clean glasses, and before he can start loading them onto the shelf, I grab one and get back to work. This is gonna be a wash, rinse, repeat kind of night.

During the following hour we maneuver around each other like we're practicing the tango. I'm ducking under his arms to get glasses while he's grabbing bottles from the shelves. Several times we reach for the ice together, and more than once, our eyes lock for a second, creating so much heat I'm surprised there's ice left. Twice I feel his hand brush my waist as I shift past him to collect empty trays from the end of the bar, sending a cascade of goose bumps down my spine.

I turn to grab a bottle of tequila from the top shelf. I do what I always do when presented with a vertical challenge—I jump/climb. *Yeah, it's a thing,* ask anyone. Wedging the toe of my sneaker into the gap between the fridges, I use the leverage to kind of jump myself up enough where I can almost reach the bottle I need.

But then I'm pinned against the back bar by a solid wall of muscle.

"Can't have you pulling the whole shelf down, can we?" Alex's warm breath tickles my ear as he stretches over my head and easily removes the bottle my fingertips barely brushed, dropping it into my open hand.

I slide down to the ground. Or maybe I melt because Alex is still pressed against me and. It's. Hot.

Not temperature hot. Really fucking sexy, my-entire-body-may-combust *hot*.

Even with my back to his chest, I can tell he's basically Thor. He removed his thick sweater when he went to sit down, and now he's only wearing a very thin, very soft plaid shirt—the type where the buttons slip from the buttonhole because it's so worn.

And he's totally ripped.

I lean into him a sliver of a fraction, but it's enough to tell there's at least an eight-pack of stacked abs underneath. Maybe ten. Dunno, whatever, it's a lot.

Stacked abs, rock-hard pecs, and thick biceps.

His head is dipped, his lips are centimeters away from my ear, but before I can move, his chest expands with a deep breath.

He's smelling me. *Smelling* me.

Oh my gawwwd.

It shouldn't be sexy, but it is. Even though it's a thousand degrees in here, and I *know* I'm gross, *and* sweaty, *and* my hair is stuck to my face, *and* beads of sweat are rolling down between my shoulder blades. It's so fucking sexy.

If I turn around, there's a good chance I'll rip his clothes off and ride him until I have to be hoisted off as my legs no longer function. And I can't do that, because have I mentioned we're far too busy tonight?

Instead, I manage to mutter, "Thanks," and slink to the side so I don't have to look at him. Or, more accurately, he doesn't see my tongue hanging from my mouth.

"You're welcome." He chuckles and moves back to his section of the bar.

We soon reach the point in the night when the floor is sticky enough that our shoes squeak with every step, but on the plus side it's definitely getting quieter—customer wise, not from the band, which is still blasting out Christmas country classics.

I turn to Alex as he lets out a roar of laughter. "What's so funny?"

He nods over to where he'd been sitting. "My brothers."

I realize I haven't been paying as much attention to them since Alex has been next to me, and glancing over, I can see their table seems to have merged with a table of girls…maybe a bachelorette. Whoever they are, they outnumber the boys two to one. One of the twins has a girl on his knee and it looks like they're playing poker, or he's teaching her how to play poker…and she's laughing right along with him nestled into his chest with a coy little smile on her face.

A weird curling sensation twists in my belly.

I can't quite figure it out—whether I'm jealous that these girls get to have fun and live their life, or that I hate they slot right in with Alex and his brothers in a way I never will.

I'm twenty-five and I've spent every waking moment of my adult life paying off debts. I don't get to be carefree and party, because I have to be up every morning to work. I've never resented my pops for what he did, but right now I kind of do. I'm working in this bar because I need the tips.

I turn to Alex, who's watching them, his face creased in amusement, and I honestly don't know why he's here when he could be over there with his brothers and those girls.

"You should go and join them, I got this now. Everyone will head out to the clubs soon, and it'll quiet down," I shout over to him. "Thanks for the help. I appreciate it."

He stares at them for a couple of seconds, and I wonder if he didn't hear me, but then his blue eyes flick to mine and he shakes his head. "No, I'm very happy right where I am."

He picks up a new order and gets back to work.

I keep expecting him to change his mind, especially when his brothers and the bachelorettes all get up to leave together. There's hardly anyone in The Old Saloon now, just one other table drinking up. The band is done, food stopped being served an hour ago, and the kitchen is closed down for the night. Boone and Jocelyn have started cleaning behind the bar, and the floor staff are helping to empty the trash and take it outside to the dumpsters.

By the time the nine of them have got their coats on and stood up, they're the only ones left. The twin stays firmly wrapped around the girl who was on his lap and guides her over to the bar. He places Alex's coat and sweater on the counter.

"Al…we're going to the Caribou Club. Come on, let's go…Haven, you're coming too," he orders, like I can drop everything and leave, and it never occurred to him otherwise.

I imagine very few people ever say no to him. If they do, I doubt it's for long. Once you've been given the full combination of those dimples, megawatt Hollywood smile, and the pleading of his deep blue eyes, you'd give him whatever he's asking for.

Except Alex, it seems. "No…I'm good here."

Twin rolls his eyes. "Al…seriously, enough playing bar manager…come and play with us. Lando's coming too."

Alex's attention flicks over to Lando, who's trying his best to edge away from the grip of the girl nearest to him by inching closer to the other twin. He's gone back to looking serious and like he'd rather be anywhere else than heading to the Caribou Club.

"I'm staying here and helping Haven."

I spin around to Alex, baffled by his insistence to stay. I hate cleaning up, and I'm paid to do it. No one does it for free. "Oh, you don't have—"

"I'm *staying*. Miles, I'll catch up with you later."

"You'd better," Miles replies, throwing me a wink. "Bye, Haven. Come and join us, make sure you bring Alex."

With that, they all leave, though I swear Lando turns around to Alex with an almost pleading look on his face before he's tugged outside by the girl next to him. And now the bar is empty…quiet. Peaceful, almost. Before anyone gets the idea that we're still open, I hurry over to bolt the doors.

I can hear Jocelyn and Boone somewhere in the cellars, checking the kegs and counting the liquor bottles to see how much we sold tonight. Based on the number of trash cans I saw being taken down there, it's a lot. They'll be there a while.

Alex is leaning against the bar, propped on one elbow, and there's a look on his face I can't read. But that thick, heavy tension between us is back, and this time, it feels like it's pushing out all of the oxygen in the room. My heart is hammering hard in my chest.

God's honest truth. This guy is *the hottest guy* I've ever seen in my life.

I need a drink.

I manage to unstick my tongue from the roof of my mouth and swallow. "You want a drink. Eggnog?"

"Fuck no." He chuckles.

I clutch the bottle he helped me lift down and wave it. "Tequila?"

"Yeah. Tequila."

I fill two glasses with ice and a squeeze of lime, pour it over, and slide one to him. Though he's stepped nearer to me, so it almost slides past him before he catches it with one big hand.

"Thank you for coming to my rescue tonight."

"You're welcome. It's the least I could do

after you saved me from the Christmas music the other night."

I roll my lips, so tempted to ask him why he hates Christmas. Because how can someone *hate* Christmas? But it doesn't feel like the right time. Instead, I say, "So we're even then."

He picks up his drink and sips, his throat working as he swallows. I need all the ice in my glass to cool me down.

His blue eyes bore into mine. "Yeah, we're even."

It's a thousand times hotter and sweatier than it was before, even though it's now empty except for the two of us. There's a faint clatter in the distance, I have no idea where anyone's got to. I'm *alone* with this guy.

My brain is completely fogged, but I know I'm not imagining this chemistry. It was there by the jukebox two nights ago, then my shop, then the bakery. That's three separate occasions with chemistry. I'm definitely *not* delusional.

And now there's enough electricity sparking

here to light the continental United States.

He places his glass down and steps closer, leans in *a little closer*…and his eyes flick up to the giant ball of mistletoe I made Joe hang above the bar.

I can't stop myself. I grip the front of his shirt and tug him into me. I can't tell if his mouth crashes to mine first or if I lift on my tiptoes to get there *right* before he does, but I forget all about it when his tongue sweeps into my mouth.

Wet, hot, zero inhibitions. The way you kiss someone for the first time when you know you're probably never going to see them again. When there's *nothing* to lose. A big hand wraps around my waist and lands on my ass, yanking me flush with his solid body. Fingers push through the sweaty strands of hair at the base of my neck and grip onto my ponytail.

He pulls my head back just enough to give him more access, his tongue thrusting harder down my throat.

I can taste tequila and lime. I can smell the oaky, earthy scent he wears. It's delicious. *He's* delicious.

Gripping onto me, he lifts me up, sits me on the top of the bar, and nestles himself between my thighs, all without his mouth ever breaking contact, and I can't help it…the loudest groan escapes me. Loud enough that he pauses for a fraction of a second and chuckles.

My palms ghost over the stubble coating his face, soft and scratchy all at the same time, and push into his hair. It's so silky and thick, I can picture myself gripping onto it while his face is between my legs, and then Alex clasps my ass in his hands, tugs me to the edge of the bar, and grinds against me.

Ho-ly. Fuck. This guy is *enormous*.

Images of him naked flash before me. He's nothing short of incredible, and I'm nothing but a sopping wet, panting mess sitting on the bartop.

At least I haven't cleaned it yet.

My hands push under his shirt and slip along

his smooth, bare back. At the same time, he tilts my hips for another grind of his, making sure the friction we get is *just right*. It's been a while since I dry humped anyone, and I do not remember it being this good.

"Fuck, I wanna get you naked," he mutters into my mouth. "Come back with me."

His tongue plunges into my mouth again, and I can't think of any good reason why not. No reason at all why we shouldn't already be in the car on the way back to his. Maybe fucking in the car.

He's probably got a big car.

Alex mutters my name. I *know* I moan.

"Haven? Haven. You up there?"

Oh *shit*.

I push Alex away and jump off the bar seconds before Jocelyn pops her head around the door leading to the cellar. I'm going to ignore the look on her face and pretend that she hasn't guessed exactly what's been going on, especially as I'm catching my breath and

Alex is straightening himself up over in the corner.

"Hey…yeah…we're just cleaning the bar… um, tables. What's up?" I pick up a nearby cloth as evidence of said cleaning.

Her eyes flick to Alex, who's pulling his sweater on, and back to me. "Do you have the key for the hatch? We need to get the empty kegs out."

I pat myself down before I realize that they're behind the bar. "Yeah, I'll bring them to you."

"Okay, thanks." She smirks. "We're restocking the shelves."

"Cool. Cool. Great idea."

When she leaves, I turn back to Alex, who's standing near the door, all straightened up, although I can see an impressive bulge in his jeans. It takes him four large strides before he's back in front of me and pulling on my ponytail so I'm looking up at him.

Now I'm not sitting on the bar, I can fully appreciate just how big he is.

How *tall* he is.

I'm not short, but he's still towering over me. And for the first time ever, I feel…small.

"Come back with me. I'll wait for you." His gaze scours my face, and I heat up all over again. "Come back to mine so I can get you naked."

I'm so tempted. God, am I *sooo* tempted. But I have to be awake in six hours to open the bakery, and while it might be presumptuous of me to think we'd be having sex *all* night, we'd definitely be having sex all night.

Reluctantly, I shake my head. "Thanks, but I need to stay and finish up here. And I have to open the bakery. Rain check?"

Alex nods as if understanding, though he seems to be disappointed. "Okay. I guess I'll see you tomorrow morning."

"Tomorrow morning?"

He unbolts the door, and a blast of cold, fresh air shoots into the bar.

"Yes." He turns and winks. "I need to get more cinnamon buns."

Merry Christmas

Alexander

8

I can categorically say I've never woken up earlier than the sun and sprung out of bed with the same amount of enthusiasm my nephew has when he's been promised ice cream, but here I am.

Sex is a powerful motive.

Except I arrive so early to collect the cinnamon buns that the bakery isn't open yet, and I have to stay in the car to wait. It was so early that Haven walked past the car, and I ducked down so she wouldn't see me.

There's a strong scent of sugar

wafting through the air, even with the windows closed, and the queue outside the bakery has quickly snaked around the corner, almost to where I'm parked. A man who looks like he's about to head on a North Pole expedition is standing right in front of the car, while everyone else is wrapped up and ready for a day in the mountains. Several of them are carrying large boxes for what I assume is to take home their purchases—the bakery equivalent of a reusable shopping bag.

They look like they mean business. I look… well…Miles would call me a loser…I'd prefer to use the term *go-getter.*

Because I think that's what I'm doing. I'm getting…

Cinnamon buns? Definitely. Coffee? Absolutely. Haven? With any luck.

She's the only reason I'd be out of bed *this* early on holiday. It's not even seven.

In fact, if I was only given a choice of one thing to get, I'd pick Haven. Because since last night, she's literally all. I. Can. Think. About.

I *know* if I'd taken her home with me last night like I'd wanted to, I wouldn't now be sitting in my car trying to keep warm. Nope. I'd be warm enough and balls deep inside what I can only imagine is the sweetest pussy in existence. It has to be. There's no way Haven would have anything else.

But sadly, instead of enjoying a night with her in my bed, I left her in the bar, arrived home to empty, semidarkness, and jumped into a cold shower. I needed to make myself come twice before I could calm the raging hard-on I'd been sporting since I'd kissed her.

When I woke up thinking about her, I'd repeated it all again—to the image of her kneeling in front of me, her full lips wearing that berry-red lipstick wrapped around my cock as I fed it down her throat. It was followed by the visual of bending her over, my fingers digging into her full, voluptuous arse, and fucking her until she screamed my name.

I can't remember the last time I had a

connection like this with someone. Maybe it's the mountain air and the prospect I won't see her again after Saturday. Based on the ferocity of her moans I swallowed while her tongue was down my throat, I'd say Haven was of the same opinion.

If we hadn't been interrupted, I'd have fucked her on the bar.

With any luck, I can pick up where we left off. I told her I'd see her this morning, and I'm nothing if not a man of my word.

The guy next to the car steps away and I realize the bakery's been opened up. Show time. Zipping up my thick puffer coat and pulling on my beanie, I hop out and immediately regret it.

Jesus Christ. I'm sure it wasn't this cold yesterday. No wonder Arctic Expedition Guy is dressed like that. This is what happens when you get into the car from the comfort of a heated garage. I don't even question my sanity, because I'm too cold to think.

Miraculously, the queue moves quickly and I'm only standing outside for five minutes before

I reach the store entrance. I'll hand it to the people in front of me, they weren't messing around when they decided to come here. They knew what they wanted—mostly the cinnamon buns and coffee from the looks of everyone on their way out—paid, and left.

My eyes are already trained on Haven as I step inside. She's filling the shelves behind the counter with her back to the customers. Today, a pink apron is hugging those curves I dug into last night, and unlike every other time I've seen her, her hair is down, tumbling over her shoulders, and even from where I'm standing behind ten patrons still waiting to be served, I can tell it's still damp.

And that fact *does something to me* because now all I can think about is whether she was doing the same thing in the shower this morning that I was, and what she looks like when she comes.

The guy in front of me turns around and frowns like he can hear my thoughts.

I really fucking hope he can't.

He stares so long that I'm about to ask what his problem is, but then the queue moves, and the pull of sugar is too strong for him to resist. He buys up what's left of the cinnamon bun tray, and from his narrowed side eye at me, I swear it's only because he thinks that's what I want too.

What a dick.

Before I can think any more about it, he steps to the till and now it's my turn at the counter. Haven's friend/colleague looks at me, and I know from her grin that *she* knows exactly who I am. And she *knows.*

"Was it warm in your car?"

"What?" I ask, in response to her strange question.

"You were sitting in your car when Haven and I arrived this morning. We were going to say hi, but it looked like you were hiding." She smirks. "You're no James Bond, though. You know that, right?"

If I could roll my eyes without her seeing, I would. But, whatever.

The friend crosses her arms over her chest. "So, another four of everything? Or are you only here to see Haven?"

Obviously I was going to be getting cinnamon buns, but from the way her eyes narrow at me, I feel like she's expecting more.

"Just give me what you have," I mutter, because at least I can throw money at the problem and save face, but her grin widens.

"Haven…you got a visitor," she yells way louder than she needs to.

Everyone in the bakery turns to look at me, even the ones who were on the way out.

This time I roll my eyes right at the friend. "*Thanks*."

"You got it, pal."

Grabbing Haven's arm, she thrusts an empty cake box at her and switches their positions so that she takes over Haven's job of restocking the shelves and Haven is in front of me. There's a swipe of icing sugar across her brow, which I refrain from wiping off, and

I realize the dick in front of me who took all the cinnamon buns actually did me a favor because now I have an excuse to hang around while more are brought out.

"Hey." I smile.

Fuck, I like that blush of hers. The rosy pink that spreads across her cheeks like a sunrise. I like it a lot. I wonder if it's *everywhere*.

Haven's green eyes widen in surprise. "Alex… what are you doing here?"

"Told you I'd come in for cinnamon buns," I reply, and there's something about the way she flusters that boldens my resolve. "Plus, I wanted to see you. Maybe make a little plan for later, if you're free."

"Oh…" She does one of those weird little curtseys again, before her hands fly to her face. "Oh my god, I don't know why I do that. It's like the worst nervous tick ever."

Leaning forward, I lower my voice. "I make you nervous?"

"No…yes. No. *No.* You don't." her mouth is

held in a tight line, but only to stop a smile from breaking.

"Good, because I didn't make you nervous last night."

Her teeth drag against her bottom lip, and my dick swells.

"No, you didn't." She peers up at me under her thick lashes, and she's remembering exactly how I didn't make her nervous. "It's the English thing. I've never been to England, so I have it in my head that you're all related to the king or something. I've watched too much *Downton Abbey*."

I decline from giving her an explanation of the British peerage system, and telling her that my mother's side of the family *is* related to the king. Mostly because I'd sound like a complete twat if I did, but also because it's boring as fuck. Instead, I just laugh along with her, because her laugh is infectious and I don't want it to stop.

"I guess it's the same as me watching

too much *Yellowstone* and pretending I'm Kevin Costner."

"Yeah." She grins. There's a beat before she continues, "Cowboys are hot, though."

"Are they?" I tilt my head as I look at her. "Do you ride?"

I may as well have *double entendre* flashing in neon above my head.

She huffs a little laugh, and her cheeks go bright pink. I expect her to look away, but she doesn't.

"I do..." she replies eventually, and a glint of amusement sparks in her eye. Yeah, she's definitely as into this as I am. "Though I haven't in a while."

I hold her gaze. I haven't been cold since I stepped into the store, but now I'm on the verge of breaking a sweat. I expect her to blink, but her green eyes widen in challenge, and I'm fairly certain I'm succeeding in organizing a hookup before seven thirty in the morning.

Stick that in your pipe, Miles.

"We should rectify that."

Her pupils dilate a fraction. "We *should*."

Haven's still holding an empty cake box, and I have no intention of breaking this insane tension between us by asking her to fill it. Instead, one of the chefs does it for us, busting through the swing doors carrying a large tray with a very intricate gingerbread house on it.

"Wow, the chefs are really getting good at those."

He places it on the shelf behind the counter next to another one, and for the first time I notice how many there are. All different, all bloody good. Most of them have been decorated with all the colored candy and licorice they have in America, but this new one is another level.

Haven shakes her head. "No, they were brought in yesterday. It's for the competition."

My brows drop until I'm almost squinting, while my mouth hangs open. I point to the new gingerbread addition. It's hard to call it a house, because it's not really a house, it's more like a gingerbread mansion…no, gingerbread chalet. The tray is covered in cotton wool for snow, and the whole thing looks like a maquette of Aspen Village, with a backdrop of mountains, trees, snowmen, and a ski lift…a fucking *ski lift. Made of gingerbread.*

It's not cutesy or covered in candy canes. In fact, there's so much detail on it, it could take the front page of *Architectural Digest*.

"*That?* Someone made *that? How?* It's a thousand times better than the one the chef made yesterday."

I turn back to the table where the one from yesterday is still sitting, looking bland as fuck. It's a donkey stable in comparison.

Haven nods.

"*That* was made from the same kit we have?" I don't believe it. There's no way.

"Yep." A smile lights her face, and for a second, I forget how flabbergasted I am, because her smile is entirely distracting. "I told you we're a competitive bunch. That's the Rivern family's entry, they come over from New York every winter, and they've won the past three years. Entries are only judged on the actual house, but they always like to create a story. Last year they set it in London, and the house was Buckingham Palace."

Glancing back to the shelf, I decide there's no way the Rivern family don't plan six months out. You can't just make that on a whim, it's way too professional.

It seems I've severely underestimated this gingerbread thing, and there's work to be done. Yesterday I thought it was a bit of a joke, and now I'm not so sure. I'm no patisserie chef, but there hasn't been a Burlington in existence who's not risen to a challenge…and it seems there's no limit. The Rivern family will need to settle for second place this year.

The queue is still growing, and Haven takes my silent thoughts as an opportunity to pack up some of the fresh cinnamon buns, which were just brought out. But time is now of the essence. I swirl a finger around the box she's sealing up.

"Okay, leave it at that. But add another eight house kits."

"Eight?"

"Eight," I reply with conviction, my chin jerking to the shelf. "We need spares. If *that's* the level I'm against, I'm not taking any chances."

"Okaaaay."

I can see she thinks I'm nuts. There's a quiver on her lip that doesn't drop as she fetches them and rings it all up. But what she doesn't know is that once I decide I want something, very little will stop me. I want her. And I want to win this competition.

I tap my Amex against the reader. "So, where are we meeting later, once I've spent the afternoon decorating gingerbread? You don't want to help me, do you? Or is that against the rules?"

"Sorry…I've got Christmas trees to sell." She grins. "But I can do a drink later."

"Sounds perfect. Seven at The Old Saloon?"

She shakes her head. "No, there's another place called Moonshine. It's on the next block over, a little farther down in the direction of the river. I'll meet you there. It's cozy, and dark."

"Cozy and dark is good." I lean in and take the bags from her, stopping short of kissing her like I want to. But I see her breath hitch just the same. "Seven it is."

I turn around when I reach my car, and through the window, I can still see her smiling.

Merry Christmas

Alexander

9

I kick the Range Rover door shut. It's taken two trips to the car to bring all the shopping bags in, even with one hooked on each finger.

For a brief second, I think my mother's flown over because her voice is the first thing I hear as I walk into the house. Then I breathe a sigh of relief when I see Lando standing in front of the vast glass windows next to Miles's tree, holding his phone out.

Don't be mistaken, I love my mother. But the Duchess of Oxfordshire and Aspen wouldn't be a great match.

She likes her snow in Gstaad or St. Moritz. Though she'd probably find refuge in Chanel.

He turns around as he hears my footsteps and throws me a deep roll of his eyes. He's clearly been standing there for a while, and from the sounds of it, it's *still* going to be a while before he gets a word in.

"James can organize for all of Caroline's things to be bagged up and sent to the charity shop."

"Mum—"

"And to think I welcomed her into our family."

I cover a snort.

Welcoming isn't the adjective I'd have used to describe her behavior toward Caroline, but then again, it would be easier to welcome a pit viper. Dropping the shopping bags, I perch on the end of the table and listen, because if I'm not mistaken, Lando has *finally* told our mother exactly why the wedding was called off, and not just because "they got cold feet." Probably wise having an entire continent between us when he did.

"Mum, stop talking, will you? Let Caroline

collect her things and leave. I don't want you getting involved. You don't need to get involved."

"I'm already involved, darling. I'm your *mother*."

"I'll do it," Clemmie interrupts, her voice loud enough that it echoes. "It won't take me long, I'll go to Bluebell Cottage, pack it all up, and text her to collect them."

Lando's shoulders drop in relief. "Thanks, Clem."

"You're welcome."

"You can move back into Burlington, darling. Bluebell Cottage is too small for you anyway, I don't know why you insisted on living there. Burlington is your birthright. We'll redecorate the cottage, new furniture, and it can be rented out. Just like all the other cottages in Valentine Nook."

Lando runs his finger over his brow and sighs again, but doesn't put up an argument, so I jump in.

"Wow, mum, an entire redecoration? Just buy a new mattress, it'll be easier."

That raises a smile on Lando, but only a small one, and it's more because he knows I'm trying to get our mother riled up. Which it does.

"Don't be ridiculous, Alexander," she snaps. "It's overdue for an upgrade, anyway."

"If you're redecorating, can you do mine, too, then? And Miles's could do with one, though his probably needs a hazmat team."

Clemmie chuckles, but the sharp tut comes straight from Mum.

"Has everything calmed down at home now?" I ask, swiftly before she starts talking about paint swatches.

"Yes, it's fine. Though I do wish you'd told me about *her* sooner. The press release went out on the day of the wedding, and we have no intention of saying anything more. Everyone will get bored eventually. They've left the village for the moment."

"Thanks, Mum. I'm sorry about it all, truly."

There's a weariness in Lando's voice I feel deep in my bones.

"You've got nothing to be sorry about, darling. At least it's given the press something other than Miles to write about for once." I can almost see her pursing her lips.

Lando rolls his eyes, even though it's true. Miles is in the papers more often than not, and much to our mother's chagrin, it has less to do with his skills on the polo field as part of the England team, and more to do with his skills in the bedroom.

"Al…" Clemmie cuts in, and once more our mother is stopped in her tracks. "I want to hear more about this Christmas tree girl."

This time I groan. Thankfully Lando takes one look at my face and decides now is the time to end the call. "Sorry, both, Al will need to tell you another day. The car's here to take us to the slopes."

I turn to look out of the front windows. There's nothing there. Not to mention we're not skiing today. We have a gingerbread competition to win, and Miles is playing a snow polo tournament tomorrow, so we're going down to look at the ponies later.

"Oh, okay, darling. Love you both. Please don't do anything silly."

Loosely translated that means to keep a close eye on Miles. Something easier said than done.

"Don't worry, Miles is still in one piece, and he's having an early night tonight." Lando grins wide. "Bye, Clem. Love you."

I barely get out a "Bye" myself before Lando shuts the phone off and tosses it onto the nearby couch.

"So…you told Mum the full story, then?"

Pushing his hands into his pockets, he rocks back on his heels and nods sadly. "Yeah. Easier than I expected. I didn't realize quite how much she really hated Caroline."

I chuckle, not that it's *that* funny, because it definitely made things hard for Lando. But no one liked her, some were just better at hiding it than others. Me, for instance, and Hendricks.

"What did she say?"

"Thank god we never gave her any of the family jewels." Lando mimics our mother's voice perfectly, before his face drops again. "As far as Mum is concerned, Caroline can keep what she was given and use it as a payoff."

And by my calculation, that comes to a couple of million.

"All in an honest day's work." I laugh. "And you'll probably get a week's grace before Mum starts trying to set you up again."

"Don't." He groans, though his jaw is clenched in frustration, because he knows it's true.

Our mother won't stop until all her children are married and producing babies. At least when Max came along for Hendricks, it calmed her urge to become a grandmother, but it's Lando's job to produce an heir to Burlington, and she doesn't let him forget it.

"Have you heard from Caroline?"

He picks up his phone from where he tossed it, opens it up, and hands it to me. My eyes scan down the screen, widening with every message I read.

There have to be over fifty from Caroline, all with some iteration of *I'm sorry, it was a mistake.*

Not one has been replied to.

"Shit," I hiss. "What about Jeremy?"

He nods to his phone, so I scroll through more until I see Jeremy's name. There's just one message, sent in the early hours before the wedding.

Jeremy:
Sorry, mate, I know I've fucked up our friendship. But I'm in love with her.

This time, I let out a low whistle.

"Jesus. I didn't see that plot twist."

"Nope."

"This must have been going on for ages."

His head bobs, sad and resigned. "Yup."

"I don't know if that makes this whole situation better or worse." I toss the phone back onto the sofa.

"Me either. It's all I've been thinking about. How long had it been going on? Did I see the signs and ignore them? Why didn't I notice?"

"What've you come up with?"

He drags a hand down his face and drops into one of the big chairs with a heavy sigh. "Fucking nothing."

"Well, you don't have to do anything about it now. But maybe you should move back into Burlington, you're going to have to eventually."

"Yes, I know," he replies. "I only moved out because Caroline didn't want to live so close to Mum, even though she's in a completely different wing of the house."

I nod. As shit as breaking up before a

wedding is, it's clear to anyone with eyes that Lando's had a lucky escape.

"You'll be closer to the day-to-day operations," I reason, though it's a weak argument. With a pair of binoculars on a clear day you can see the top of Bluebell Cottage from Burlington.

"By what? A couple of fields?"

"The other bonus is that you never have to hear Miles talking about your CaNdo Attitude." I laugh, because Miles, being Miles, decided to give Caroline and Lando a celebrity-style moniker. One they both hated, therefore Miles used it whenever he could.

I watch a broad smile spread across my brother's face; it turns into a grin, which turns into a big belly-rumbling laugh. "There's the silver lining if I ever saw one. That *fucking* name."

"Thought you'd be happy."

"So happy." He sits up and peers at the dozen bags I dropped on the floor when I arrived back. "What's that? Where've you been?"

I'm just about to reply when the small side

door opens and out walks Maggie. She's carrying a huge tray laden with coffees, pancakes, scrambled eggs, and bacon. After all the flurry of this morning, I suddenly realize I am absolutely famished.

"Good morning, sirs. I thought you might like your breakfast out here this morning." She says, placing the tray on the large table as Lando leaps up to help her.

"Thank you, Maggie. Great idea. This is perfect."

"You're welcome." She smiles, though it's not as big of a smile as Miles usually gets, and she leaves without saying another word—but only once she's had a good look around and not spotted Miles.

"I think she was hoping you were someone else." I laugh and grab a cup to pour a coffee. "Where are the terrible two, anyway? How was the Caribou Club?"

Lando's busy spooning heaps of scrambled egg onto his plate and shrugs without looking up. "Didn't go."

"You came back on your own?"

He nods and takes the coffee I pass him. "I think I heard them get in around four a.m. and they weren't alone."

"What?" I ask, picking up a slice of crispy bacon and crunching down on it.

"The twins…they came back with girls."

"Ahh. Only a matter of time, I s'pose."

"Exactly." He puts down his plate, now loaded with toast, scrambled eggs, bacon, and pancakes. "So are you going to tell me why you were at…" he peers at the shopping bags, "…Trader Joe's before eight a.m.?"

"Gingerbread house competition," I reply, buttering a slice of toast. "Has to be in by Thursday, we've got two days."

"I'm going to need you to expand with a little more information. I wasn't listening to Miles yesterday when he was banging on about it. If we have to make the gingerbread, I think we need to opt out. It's not really safe to let any of us loose in the kitchen. Except Hendricks."

He's right, Hendricks is the only one of us who can legitimately cook.

"No, we don't have to make the gingerbread."

And I proceed to tell him about the competition, along with everything I saw this morning in the bakery, including the Rivern Family's entry of Aspen Village.

"I'm all on board for winning a competition, but what exactly are we going to be making?" he asks.

I shrug. "Haven't got that far, we need to brainstorm. It needs to be good, better than Aspen Village, that's for sure. *Rivern brownnosers.*"

Lando lifts a thick eyebrow. "And this is all to do with the girl you ditched us for last night? The Christmas tree girl, who also works in a bakery? What's her name again?"

I glance up to find my oldest brother looking at me with amusement thick set on his face. I could lie and say no, it's about winning—especially as the only reason we came to Aspen in the first place was to get him away from England and his cheating fiancée. It's not ideal I've met a girl when I should be supporting him.

"Haven. And yes, kind of," I say eventually.

"What happened last night?"

"Not as much as I wanted to…" I smirk, swiping the last bit of my pancake through the maple syrup on my plate.

"If you make your gingerbread house well enough, you could be in with a chance…"

"I'm in with a chance anyway. I'm meeting her later for drinks. Somewhere dark and cozy…" I grin, and my dick twitches. "Winning at this is an added bonus. Plus, it's for charity." I pause for a second as a pang of guilt makes itself known. "D'you mind?"

"Mind what?"

"Mind if I…you know…"

"Hook up with a girl?"

"Yes. If you'd rather I stayed here with you—"

He's about to reply, but there's a clatter on the stairs behind us and we both turn to see Miles with his arm around a blonde girl. On closer inspection, it's not an affectionate arm around her, it's more in the style of trying to hurry her along. It would account for Miles's eye roll and why *he's* carrying *her* shoes plus a tiny gold bag, and why he doesn't notice Lando and me before she does.

"Ooh, is that coffee?"

I'm about to offer her some just to annoy Miles, but he distracts her with a kiss that lasts far too long for this time of the morning and opens the front door. A gust of freezing air whirls in. Lando's eyebrows shoot up because, aside from an enormous fur bomber jacket and what looks like the shortest skirt known to man, she's not wearing anything else.

"Bye, sweetheart. Last night was fun… shame I have to go back to England."

"But I'm coming to watch you play tomorrow, don't forget," the blonde squeaks, trying to keep warm.

She's now peering around Miles, even though he's doing his best to block her view by hopping up and down as he pulls on a pair of snow boots. It's quite the entertainment, especially when Miles shoots us a scowl and slams the door behind them.

"At least he's walking her to the gate," mutters Lando, as I chuckle. "Not sure that's happened before."

"Perhaps he's matured. It's been a while since we were privy to the Miles Burlington morning parade." I pick up my coffee and sit back. "Mum really should get started on settling him down, it's going to take a decade as it is."

Lando's still laughing when Miles returns from seeing the blonde into what I hope was an Uber.

"What's so funny?" he asks and cups his hands together to breathe warmth into them.

"Just talking about Mum working on finding you a wife."

Miles stops midstride and visibly shudders. "Hard pass."

"Did you not want to introduce us to your new friend?"

"Not especially," he responds, snatching up a piece of bacon before dropping into the chair at the end of the table. "Where's the coffee?"

"In front of you."

Miles's gaze drops to the pot and he reaches for a cup. "So it is."

Lando and I quietly sip our coffee, while Miles slowly peers around at the offering on the table, and his eyes light up.

"Wait. Are those fresh cinnamon buns? From the bakery?" A shit-eating grin spreads across his face and he pins me with a look that should come with devil horns. "Alex*ander*..."

"Yes."

"You dirty dog."

"Says the guy who just shoved a girl out the front door into the cold without even offering her a to-go cup of coffee."

"They know the deal with me. You, however…" He wags his finger at me.

"Doesn't sound like she knows the deal… two days in a row," teases Lando. "Or are you slacking? How are you going to get out of her coming to the polo?"

"There's going to be a thousand people there. She won't be allowed with the players," he replies simply, because he's well practiced in avoiding women.

"Is Henners awake yet?" I ask, pushing my coffee cup over to him to top up.

"Yeah, he's talking to Max."

Hendricks's life revolves around his son, Maxwell.

Max might not have been planned, but since the day he came into all our lives, he's never known anything other than unconditional love. It's unfortunate that Max's mother isn't the mother he deserves and was more interested in Hendricks's money than having a child, but now Hendricks has full custody it's brought a stability that Max didn't have before, and they're rarely apart. I know it's been hard for him to be away from his son this week, but I also know that he would do anything to support Lando. He's still going to be first on the plane home though.

I yawn and check my watch. Hendricks is going to be a while.

"We don't have to be down at the polo club until two. I'm going in the hot tub, and then we've got time for a ski. Haven't taken my board out yet," says Miles, reading my expression incorrectly. I'd kind of like all four of us here when I explain about the gingerbread.

"Nope. Not this morning. I have other plans for you."

His skeptical gaze slices between Lando and me. "What plans?"

"Al's decided we're going to win the gingerbread competition."

"Seriously?"

"Yup," I reply, and gathering up as many bags as I can carry, I deposit them at the clear end of the table.

"What's all this?"

"Decorating stuff."

"For the gingerbread house," adds Lando. "Haven—"

Miles winces and looks up at me with eyes full of pity. "Al, this is a lot of effort just to get laid. If you need me to give you tips…"

Lando barks out a laugh.

My jaw clenches. "Fuck's sake."

I lay everything out on the table, all neatly compartmentalized in sections, and turn back to my brothers.

The younger one peers at me over the top of his coffee cup. "All right, Alexander, I'm in. I'm very much enjoying this less Grinchy version of you we've seen the past few days. So if I have to decorate a Christmas cookie or whatever to keep you smiling and get some, then I'll do it."

"*Thanks.*" I roll my eyes.

Once more, Miles is annoyingly correct. Now I think about it, I haven't hated *this* December quite as much as usual. I've been less edgy, more tolerant of Miles, and yesterday, Lando commented on how my melancholy wasn't quite so pronounced this year.

Maybe coming to Aspen at Christmas wasn't such a terrible idea.

Merry
Christmas

Haven

10

Haven:
I'm here too early

Saylor:
What time did you say you'd meet him?

Haven: Seven

Saylor:
It's two minutes after. How is that early?

Haven:
Because he's late

Saylor:
Did you shave your legs?

Haven:
Of course I did

Saylor:
It's about time

Haven:
Shut up

Saylor:
Lipstick?

Haven:
No

Saylor:
Good plan, it's only going to get kissed off anyway

Saylor:
Proud of you, Havey, so good you're finally getting some *eggplant emoji* *water emoji*

Haven:
Shut up

Saylor:
Don't think about it. Just do it.

Haven:
Shit, he's here, gotta go

Whoa.

Alex walks through the main doors, looking every inch like he belongs here. In Aspen, my town, where the billionaires come to play.

Shrinking back slightly into the shadows, I watch as he scans the dimly lit bar, the smattering of patrons sitting in the navy velvet booths with strategically placed table lamps, the walls adorned with antlers, and the bar staff dressed like they've spent the day making moonshine.

Every inch of my body clenches, and I resist the urge to stand up so he sees me, because I want to savor this. Savor *him* as he is, in those same dark wash jeans he was wearing the other night when he was peering over the jukebox, like they were made for him and him alone, tight ass on display.

Today he's added a navy cable-knit sweater that makes his eyes seem impossibly blue, even from where I'm sitting. Tugging off his beanie, he ruffles through his hair, perfecting that tousled look. And my body chooses this moment to remind me I've already made out with this guy. That I've already run my fingers through his hair and know exactly how soft it is.

He is *so hot.*

I appreciate the full package that is Alex... *shit, I don't know his last name*...I'm about to have sex with someone and I *don't know* his last name. *Should* I know his last name?

Another stream of incoming messages from Saylor is buzzing in my bag as Alex spots me, and a lazy smile spreads across his face that lays waste to every second thought I had about coming here tonight.

Right now I don't even want to stay for drinks.

I want to go straight back to mine and finish what we started.

"Hey there." He leans down to kiss my cheek.

And…I'm lightheaded from the closeness; the scent of him; the lingering of his cool lips against my warm skin. The anticipation.

"Hey," I manage to breathe out.

The table I chose has two sets of rounded velvet seats, each big enough to fit two or three people comfortably. I assumed Alex would sit across from me, but I find myself scooching up in mine as he slots in next to me, one big arm around the back of the chair.

He twists his body so he's right in my space, his legs touching mine, and I'm finding it hard to take more than a shallow breath. He's close enough that I can see the flecks of dark blonde in his stubble and a faint tan outline from skiing the past few days.

He gives me a lopsided grin while he properly takes in our surroundings. "I like this place. You certainly described it well. Dark and cozy, indeed. It's busy too."

I nod, stopping myself from chewing on my lip like I do when I'm nervous. "Yeah, Saylor and I come sometimes when we want to get away from The Old Saloon crowd."

"Saylor is your friend from the bakery? The chatty one?"

"Yes, the chatty one." My smile widens. "My best friend. We grew up here together. She teaches first grade in the local school, but she's helping out in the bakery during Christmas break."

"How's the competition going? Had lots of entries?" He asks, then raises his index finger. "Hang on, first we need drinks. This place looks like it makes excellent cocktails. Then I want to hear all about what I'm up against."

Alex's hand shoots in the air, and within thirty seconds a server arrives with a menu. "Haven, what would you like?"

I kind of want a beer, because the pours in this place are *generous*, and I don't want to get the kind of drunk where I end up being carried home. But I also need to take the edge off the adrenaline rushing through my body with such force I'm trembling.

In the end I panic order something that I know from experience gets me *the most drunk.*

"Old-fashioned, please."

Dear god, Haven.

"Good choice, make that two." Alex hands the menus back without ever opening them and turns to me. "I'm thankful you didn't say eggnog. Now, where were we? How was your day?"

"It was busy, it's always a busy time of year. Especially with the competition." I laugh when Alex grimaces.

"How many houses have been dropped off so far?"

"About a hundred. Tomorrow will be busier, then Thursday is chaos. No one wants to bring their house in until they have to, because they don't want anyone to see it and feel the need to cheat." I look up as the waiter returns with our drinks. "Thank you."

Alex takes both glasses and hands one to me. Blue eyes bore into mine, and it must be the low oxygen in the mountain air, because I'm finding it hard to breathe.

"To gingerbread competitions, and the prettiest mayor of Aspen I've ever met."

My glass clinks to his, my cheeks heat at the compliment, and I take far too big a sip. The burn of whiskey immediately hits my bloodstream.

"To gingerbread competitions."

Alex throws his head back with a loud laugh, his eyes flashing in amusement, and his tongue darts along the edges of his perfect, white teeth. "If anyone told me I'd be entering the world's most competitive baking contest, I'd think you were talking about *The Great British Bake Off*."

"Oh no, we're way more competitive." I giggle, putting my glass down. "It's going to be a tough crowd this year."

"I'm not worried, I have the edge."

My brows shoot up. "Oh, you think so?"

He reaches out, picks the ends of my hair off my shoulders, and curls it around his index finger. My heart stutters.

"Oh, I know so."

"Are you going to tell me what it is?"

"Nope."

Before I can stop it, he's pulling me toward him and his mouth surrounds mine. Soft lips press against me as his tongue runs along the seam of my lips until I open up. All too briefly, he sweeps around my mouth and pulls back, but not before he lets out a low moan that hits every part of my body. I cross my legs tighter and squeeze.

"Sorry, couldn't help myself."

"I hope you don't think that making out with me is going to get you any prizes."

He shakes his head. "No, I'll be the winner regardless. You, however, are going to need to control yourself once I'm crowned."

"Oh really?"

Lifting the strand of hair still wrapped around his finger, he presses his nose to it and inhales deeply. "Yes. Winning is a powerful aphrodisiac. You'd do well to remember that."

"I'll try my best. Can't say it's happened to me before, but I'll be on guard."

"Ah." His face lights up in amusement. "You haven't come across these dimples though." He takes my hand, stretches out a finger, and rubs it against the soft stubble, just over the deep ridge in his cheek. "Or the English accent."

"That's very true." I make one last swipe and drop my hand, though Alex doesn't let go. Instead, he links his fingers through mine.

The warmth of his signet ring on his pinkie seeps into my skin. Up close I can see it's a little worn, the sign of jewelry well-loved and rarely removed. There's a crest stamped into it with what looks like an angel next to a tree, underneath which are tiny letters…a word written in a language I don't understand.

"It's my family's crest," Alex says quietly, and I

look up to find him staring at me. "The cherub is symbolic to my family. And underneath is inscribed *amor principum*, which means *love is the beginning*."

"Oh, that's cute," I reply, taking a large gulp of my old-fashioned, because I'm not sure what else to say and I'm beginning to realize that Alex isn't quite like anyone I've ever met.

Not that I've met anyone with a family crest before—I'm not even entirely sure what a family crest is—except it's kind of like a fancy brand that we put on cattle, though more something I associate with old people.

But Alex isn't old.

He's around *my age*.

And fancy *and hot*. Real *hot*.

"So, what do you do in England when you're not building gingerbread houses?"

He huffs a small chuckle and shifts back slightly against the velvet. "I work with Lando, my eldest brother. It's a family business…we have land—farming land—which is a lot of work…that sort of thing…"

My brows draw together a little, Alex doesn't look like any guy I know who farms. Not one who spends their days caked in mud rescuing cows, hauling logs and hay bales, or digging roots anyway. Maybe England has a different type of farming.

"What do you do with it?"

"We focus on sustainable agriculture, and we've started the process of rewilding a percentage of our land too. Restore the ecosystems…that sort of thing." He trails off with a shrug in that way where you can tell someone doesn't want to go into details, but I want to hear more. I want to know how he does it. Ecosystem farming is the ethos of my tree business, it's how I want Wylder Ranch to exist.

"Do the twins work with you too?"

"God, no." He laughs with a shake of his head. "I think we'd kill each other. Miles anyway. Hendricks is a vet, and Miles plays polo."

My brows shoot up. "Polo?"

"Yeah, you know…bit like cricket on horseback." His mouth twitches in amusement.

"I don't think I know what cricket is, but I know what polo is. There's a club here. But you're saying that's his job? Is he good?"

"Yes, he is. Very. Plays for England." Alex nods deeply. "We went down to your polo club today, in fact. Miles is playing there tomorrow and Thursday in the snow polo tournament." He grins, his eyes lighting up with mischief. "You should come with me."

I groan. Once more my life is getting in the way of me having fun.

"I *can't,* I have to work."

"Ah yes, I forgot you were Mayor of Aspen for a second. Must keep all your subjects happy," he teases, with a wag of his finger. "Now your turn…what do you do when you're not selling Christmas trees and running the town?"

I pause, what exactly is the answer I give him? Because right now I do anything and everything I can.

"I guess…" I take a deep breath. "Not dissimilar to you. I have a small ranch on the national forest lines up the mountain. My family's ranch. It's where the trees are harvested for the holidays. And in the spring and summer, I plant all the new saplings. It takes a few years to rotate through, but it's what we've always done."

"You work with your family too?"

"Um…well, I did. It's just me now."

Alex blinks slowly. "That's a lot for one person."

Reaching for my glass, I sip, giving myself some time to think on where this conversation is headed. "It can be. But I have help…and over this spring I'm planning to create a retreat space out on a stretch of my land overlooking the valley. It's super pretty. The first retreat is happening this summer. There's a yoga group coming."

"That sounds excellent, my sister's always

trying to get me into yoga. Maybe I'll sign up and you'll be the one to finally succeed where she's failed." He chuckles, taking a long sip of his drink. "So is it your parents' ranch, their business?"

I pick at an invisible thread on my jeans. We're having such a nice time, and for once I'm sitting with someone who doesn't know my history and didn't know my parents, and I'm just *me*. Haven. Not the girl running about town who everyone knows, who everyone feels sorry for because she's all alone and trying to keep her parents' businesses running. I don't want to bring the mood down, but I look up into Alex's patiently waiting face, and I'm hit by guilt for *not* wanting to talk about them.

"Yes. It was, but…um, they died a while back. My mom first. Then my dad a few years later. So now it's mine, and I'm looking after it. Continuing what they started. The store was theirs, too, my mom set it up. They loved Christmas, and my mom loved decorating. I know it's kind of jumbly, but she was so obsessed with it I don't want to change it."

It's quiet, and I finally bring myself to look at Alex, praying he's not wearing that look people wear when they don't know what to say after they find out your parents are dead.

He isn't. It's worse almost. Alex is staring at me, unblinking, his face painted with shock. His eyes are *glistening* with tears.

Fuck. *I knew it.* I knew I'd bring the mood down.

And he's quiet because he doesn't know what to say, and I'm about to overcompensate by babbling about how it's all fine, because it's 100 percent better than awkward silence and the expression he's wearing.

"Haven…god. I'm so incredibly sorry to hear that. I know how…" He glances away and stops.

I want to take back everything I said, but before I can, he turns to face me again, and his eyes have returned once more to their usual bright blue sparkliness.

"No...you know what? We should toast your parents, for they made one hell of a daughter. She's the mayor of Aspen, and everything."

Somehow, Alex nails it better than anyone has before. The awkwardness vanishes, and one of the wait staff arrives before I can blink.

Alex swirls his finger over the table. "We'll take another round of these, and a bottle of Dom Perignon 2012." He turns to me with a smile that makes my chest hurt. "It's a good vintage for toasting parents."

I wouldn't know. I've never drunk a thousand-dollar bottle of champagne, let alone toasted my parents with it. Somewhere I can hear my dad saying he'd rather have a beer, and my mom telling him to stop talking.

By the time the server returns, I swear Alex is closer to me than he was five minutes ago. Even when he leans forward to take the champagne so he can open it himself, his knee brushes mine. I didn't get to fully appreciate it last night when he was behind the bar, but the way he eases the cork from the bottle, accentuating his big hands and thick veins running along his forearm, has me practically biting down into my lip.

I don't know how he's done it, but I've never been turned on by someone pouring me a drink before.

"Thank you," I manage to say without making it sound weird as I take the glass from him.

Alex drops the bottle back into the ice bucket and shifts nearer. The smile he gives me turns my internal temperature up another degree. I'm tempted to take one of those ice cubes and run it along my neck.

"You're welcome. Now, what were your parents called?"

"Wyatt and Jeanne."

He raises his glass. "To Wyatt and Jeanne, and the mayor of Aspen." There's a pause, then, "And to winning gingerbread competitions."

"To winning gingerbread competitions," I reply through a giggle.

Alex sips his champagne and places his glass on the table. "So, what does the Queen of Christmas Trees have at home? Do you keep the best for yourself?"

I'm about to answer, but I'm distracted by Alex once again curling my hair around his finger.

"Let me guess—it's one of those trees where nothing matches. Where all the ornaments are jumbled up, but each of them has a memory." He smiles softly, before his eyes narrow in curiosity. "And all the lights flash haphazardly in different colors with giant baubles hidden in the branches. I bet you have one for each room. Big and small."

I try to hide my amusement while also wondering if maybe I'm exactly that transparent, because he's described my trees perfectly. Except for the different colored lights. Mine are always white. My mom's were always white.

"And," he continues, his voice all tease, "I'm willing to bet a lot of money that you have an entire Father Christmas and his sleigh outside…Nooo. NO. It's on the roof, isn't it?" He scans my face, my twitching lip. "God, you have, haven't you? And you've got those nutcrackers on either side of the door."

My lips are rolled so hard together it's almost painful.

He gasps and points his finger right at me, "You have one of those houses that people come and take pictures of because of all the decorations. Don't you?"

"Hey, if it brings people joy," I say, finally.

Alex's laugh bursts out of him, loud and deep. It's infectious, genuine, and soon I'm laughing with him just as loudly. Except my eyes aren't screwed shut. I can't tear my gaze away from his face, the deep creases fanned around his eyes, or the way his wide mouth opens so the soft cupid's bow on his top lip almost disappears, and his dimples pull even further under his thick stubble.

And then our laughter kind of dies down. But the heat between us—this electricity taking hold and refusing to let either of us look away—that's turned right up, along with my pulse.

Alex's bright blue eyes drop and darken when my tongue darts out, running along my bottom lip.

"*Fuck*, I like you," he mutters, right before his lips crash to mine.

The old-fashioned and half a glass of champagne might have gone to my head, but even without it I'd still be tempted to push him back on this couch and straddle him. All from one languorous swipe of his warm tongue against mine.

The fingers twisted around my hair are now pushed up into the base of my neck as he holds me firm, his tongue moving with the exact pace I can imagine his dick easing inside me, teasing almost, an appetizer of what I have in store.

It's all credit to how good he is at kissing that I nearly forget we're in public.

Alex's free hand is curved along the inside

of my thigh, not moving, but the pressure of his fingertips torments me, something I make known when I moan into his mouth. It's breathy and pained, leaving nothing to the imagination. He pulls back from me, and the smile cresting his lips is nothing short of egotistical. An ego well earned.

The hand between my legs doesn't move as he twists around to reach his glass with his other.

"We're getting good at this." He chuckles. I'm inclined to agree.

For the next two hours we get *better*. We barely take a breath.

In between conversations about gingerbread houses and Christmas trees, skiing, and our favorite seasons—him, summer; me, Christmas, obvs—we've kissed and we've *laughed.* I've laughed more than I've laughed in years.

We've done nothing but talk, laugh, and kiss. We've kissed until it's obvious we need to take the kissing elsewhere, because I don't want it to end.

"Alex..." I half moan against his lips, desperate

not to break this connection but I'm not going to be able to contain myself much longer. One more squeeze of his hand on my thigh, or one more leisurely swipe of his tongue and we're going to get arrested for inappropriate behavior.

He pulls back and scans my face. "Back to yours?"

I'm already picking up my bag and halfway to standing. "Yeah."

Twenty minutes later we stumble through my front door, lips locked together.

Whatever's grown between us the last few days is about to explode.

Too many times I found myself wondering what it would be like to have someone like

Alex around all the time.

But Alex is a one-night thing.

Tonight is about no thinking. Just doing. Just *being*.

"I wanted to fuck you since you saved me from Christmas music," he mumbles against my lips while I'm hitting the wall for the light switch.

I know it's here somewhere.

Argh.

Bright lights blind us.

I hit it again and once more we're shrouded by the semidarkness and the twinkle of lights from the Christmas tree in the main room. The front door gets kicked shut and I'm pinned against it, Alex's big body pressing into mine.

"*Because* I saved you from Christmas music?" I half moan, because his lips are on my neck, while his hands push under my shirt, deftly unhooking my bra with the expertise of someone who's done it many times before. Even *I* don't usually get it the first time around, and it's *my* bra.

This guy's a pro.

"Yes, mostly. But also because you have an amazing pair of boobs and an arse that should be worshipped."

God, that accent is enough to get me wet, if I wasn't already. Fuck foreplay.

"Say *arse* again," I groan the order. "It sounds so dirty when you say it."

"Yeah? You like it dirty?"

"I…"

"*Arse,*" he whispers in my ear, taking my lobe between his teeth.

Forcing my arms above my head, he tugs off my shirt. I've always been kind of embarrassed about the size of my boobs, but they bounce free and I look up to Alex staring at me with nothing but pure lust. Instead of cringing with embarrassment, I'm glowing.

He reaches out, cupping one in each palm.

"Oh shiiit…" His gaze darts up to mine, and back to where his thumb is swiping over my rock-hard nipple. "Haven, they're fucking incredible."

A groan rumbles up from the pit of my core. My entire body buzzes with arousal. My brain is on sensory overload, mesmerized by the sight of what his fingers are doing.

And when it's no longer enough to touch them, he dips his head and circles his tongue around the pebbled bud.

His mouth seems to have a mind of its own, traversing across my chest, taking in one nipple at a time, leaving a hot, glistening trail of saliva and goose bumps in his wake. His hands brush down my sides to the waist of my jeans, and I can barely take a breath before he's unbuttoned them and on his knees in front of me.

Dragging them down just enough for my panties to come into view, his eyes find mine as if seeking permission before he moves any further.

I can't nod quick enough. Instead, I scrape my fingers through his hair and almost yank him into me, which seems much more polite than pushing my groin in his face. But one way or another, if I don't have this man's tongue on my clit in the next thirty seconds, I'm gonna scream. And not in the good way.

Alex needs no convincing. A dry chuckle escapes him, and one hard tug later, my jeans and panties are around my thighs. He sits back and stares, his fingers ease through the space where my thighs are clamped together, and when he pulls them out, they're covered in three hours worth of my anticipation.

Not a single part of me feels an ounce of embarrassment that I'm almost naked as he spreads me as wide as he can while I'm barely able to move, or that he's so close to me I can feel his hot breath on my pussy. Instead, I'm squirming with a desperate need for friction, trapped in a denim prison.

He remains motionless.

"Oh Haven, you're soaked. So fucking wet."

His voice is so deep and gravelly, it amps me up further. I can feel arousal dripping out of me. And when I try to take things into my own hands and move myself nearer to his face, he inches back.

My teeth almost bite through my lower lip.

"Uh-uh. Let me enjoy this. It's been a while since I saw a pussy so perfect."

I have a perfect view, too—of Alex on his knees, his thick, dark brown hair threaded between my fingers, my groin inches from his mouth as I wait for him to lean forward and taste me.

Never in a million years could I have guessed this is where we'd end up after I saw him at the jukebox.

I almost weep in need. Is it possible to die from anticipation? Asking for a friend.

"Alex, please…"

Peering up at me through glazed, hooded eyes, his mouth curved in a devilish smirk, he says nothing but leans forward and *finally* buries his face between my legs.

"I was right. You do have a sweet pussy," he mumbles, and gets to work.

"Oh…my…fuuuuck."

My head drops back against the door with a smack I barely register. All I can focus on is Alex's hot tongue dragging through my slit over and over. With each swipe, the pressure cooker that's been building since I met him is turned up another degree. This will be over embarrassingly quickly.

By the time he latches on my clit and my legs nearly buckle from under me, I'm in danger of combusting. Only his big hands clamped onto my thighs stop me from falling.

"Alex…yes, right…there."

"So fucking hot, Haven…you taste incredible…" He takes another long lap. My thighs are juddering so hard in his strong grip, I know his fingerprints will mark me for days. "You're going to come right now for me, and I'm going to watch."

This must have lasted barely ten seconds, but I still have literally no idea how I've held on *that* long.

Maybe the old-fashioneds and half a bottle

of champagne dulled my senses. All I can think is thank god they did, because there's no way I'd have managed without it. I'm so close to the edge, tears are pooling in my eyes. I need this release more than I've ever needed anything else in my life.

His fingers replace his tongue, pumping inside me as his thumb presses down hard on my clit. My eyes almost roll into my head, but I manage to focus enough to look down and see him watching me, a grin spread across his face while he licks his lips.

I'm reminded of those nature shows; he's an apex predator about to devour his kill.

That's what I am. *Kill.* I am dead. I have died.

One more precise swipe of his thumb and I crash around his fingers still working inside me. I've never felt anything like it. I've had years of practice in making myself come, a few fumbled nights of passion in between, but I've never experienced anything like this…a relentless wave crashing through me and gathering strength, ready to shred me from the inside out.

This isn't an orgasm. It's an exorcism.

Even my voice has been ripped from me. I'm only able to croak his name, "Alex."

Before my heart takes another erratic beat, his lips are on mine, his tongue plunging into my mouth. Tasting myself on his lips is the single hottest experience of my life.

But the moment is broken when we realize that I'm still stuck in the jeans he's wedged around my thighs.

"Let's remove these properly, shall we?" He laughs, but before I can wriggle out of them, I'm hauled into the air, carried across the living room, and dropped on the couch next to the Christmas tree.

Thirty seconds later, my jeans are thrown over Alex's shoulder and I'm lying naked in front of him.

He scrubs a hand down his face, his signet ring catching the light from the Christmas tree. "You're better than I ever imagined."

"All four days of it?" I giggle, my hand

shooting up to cover my mouth when it's followed by a hiccup.

He reaches behind and tugs his sweater off. "That's right. Four days of thinking of nothing but what I'd do to you when I got you naked."

I blink through the drunken haze. This can't be real. There's *no way*. I try to count, but I lose my place. What's quadrupole quadrupole? Because that's how many muscles I'm seeing.

I mean…I don't think they even make Americans like this Englishman, let alone Englishmen like him. It's not alcohol talking. This guy is a straight-up, certified god. A Christmas miracle.

"Tell me…" I find myself asking.

He glances down, his gaze slowly scanning over every inch of my body, heating it up another degree while he unbuckles his belt and kicks off his boots.

"First…" He lifts an eyebrow. "I'd be on my knees in front of you, feasting like you were my last meal. My tongue on your clit, lapping up every drop of you as my fingers got to work until you were begging for me to stop…" He pushes his jeans over his hips, hooking his thumbs into his boxer briefs, and lets them fall. "Think I accomplished that."

His cock springs free. The tip glistens. He's rock hard. And *massive.*

Oh my *god.*

I try to edge back on the couch like I need to make space for it, but he catches my leg and yanks me back.

"Don't worry, we'll make it fit."

He's full of that sly conceit as he reaches for the condom packet he pulled from the pocket of his jeans, and I can't tell if I'm turned on or scared for what's to come.

My mouth drops watching him sheath himself. He kneels on the couch next to me and shifts forward, gently griping my chin between his fingers.

The pad of his thumb runs along my bottom lip, pulling it down with a pressure

I want elsewhere. "Since the day you wore red lipstick, I've been dreaming about these wrapped around my cock. Watching you take me until I hit the back of your throat, exploding in your mouth and feeling you swallow my come."

It's less than five minutes since I experienced a mind-blowing orgasm, and I already need more. My entire body is shaking, desperate for his touch.

"I want to watch your pussy stretch around my cock as I ease into you." His hands are moving over my body, down my calf.

It's only when I wince that I remember the reason I wore jeans this evening has everything to do with the razor burn down the side of my leg that took half my skin off.

"Shit. How did you do that?" Alex kisses along where my skin is still raw.

"Shaving my legs."

"Ouch. Poor Haven." He runs his hands along my bare thigh, spreads me wider, and kneels forward. "Let's make it better."

He slides the tip of his cock through my center.

Back and forth he gently guides it around my clit.

It's the last gentle action.

One long thrust and he's inside me. All of him.

A vicious spasm runs through me. My body bows into him as he pulls out and drives back into me with a groan that vibrates over my body. I'm so full. I can't breathe, I can't focus.

I can't fit him.

I feel him everywhere.

It's too much, yet not enough.

"Fuck…look at you." The timbre of his voice licks fire across my skin. "Taking my cock…like you were born to."

I arch, and Alex's mouth finds mine, his tongue thrusting with each long drive of his hips, until I cry for surrender. I'm no match for this guy. I barely have any bones left.

Then I'm empty, missing the weight of him, the girth of him, but it only lasts a second while he hauls me up by my ass and flings my thighs over his shoulder. I'm trapped once again, this time by Alex's massive body as he leans forward and pistons himself into me.

And I lose myself.

"Alex…I'm…oh god. I'm c-c-coming."

"Yes…Haven. *Fuck.* Let me feel it," he rumbles. "Let me feel you strangling my cock."

And I do. He does. Following after me with a roar that would put a thunderstorm to shame before collapsing next to me on the couch.

I suck in as much air as I can manage in one go. "Holy…*crap.*"

"Give me a couple of minutes." He breathes out. "Then we're going again."

We fuck on the couch, the floor of my living room, the kitchen table after I went to fetch water for fear of dehydration and Alex followed, and I'm fairly certain he'll have the imprint of the stairs on his back from where he pulled me onto his lap, and I rode out orgasm number six.

Now I'm dozing. It's a semiconscious, hazy, slightly drunk state when I'm aware of movement next to me. The warm arm wrapped around me disappears. I turn to find Alex kneeling on the hardwood floor as he searches for his jeans. Easing onto my elbows, which is about as much as I can manage, I watch him pull on his boxer briefs.

We never discussed a sleepover, and honestly, I'm not sure what to do. I don't know what time it is. I just know I'm too tired to form a cohesive thought, including the etiquette of a one-night stand, but when Alex pulls on his boots, I think the decision's already been made.

"Are you leaving?"

"I have to be up early." He leans in to kiss me. The taste of me is still lingering on his lips, and I'm tempted to pull him back for another go. "See you around, Mayor of Aspen. This was fun."

I debate staying on the floor, because I'm not sure I have the strength left in my body, let alone any bones left. But in the end, I get up, force myself to walk up the stairs, and flop onto my bed.

Haven

11

I've skied my whole life, ridden horses, kayaked down the Roaring Fork River. I'm relatively fit, even if I am currently living off sugar.

But it's been two days since I had sex with Alex, and I'm *still* sore. Everywhere.

My thighs burn as I attempt to bend down and pick up a box filled with the bakery tote bags so I can refill the shelf. It's hard, but I manage.

Reaching up to thread them onto the hook? Impossible.

Don't get me started on the tree store yesterday; I could barely lift the large wreaths, let alone help anyone get a tree to their waiting cars. Customers had to help themselves.

With a loud groan, I drop the box on the counter and swipe away the hair falling in my eyes.

"Oh, come *on*. You're not still complaining about a night of amazing sex?"

I spin around to Saylor transferring a tray of Christmas cookies to the shelf. I told her about Alex yesterday morning. She wanted every little detail, and honestly, I gave it up to her. I spilled my guts like a piñata. I had to. I *needed to*. Until I spoke the words out loud, I couldn't be sure I hadn't imagined the entire evening.

Because it was *unbelievable.*

"I'm not complaining about the sex. I'm easing through the pain in my body. I'm *sore*."

She rolls her eyes. "This is why you need to have sex more often."

"Yeah, and when exactly am I supposed to

find the time?" I catch myself before I yawn, because also…I'm *tired*. And not just from the unbelievable sex.

"You make time, Haven. Like everyone." She switches the empty tray out with a full one. "Don't see me creaking around like an old lady, do you? No, because I keep myself in sex-ready shape."

My eyes roll to the heavens. "Yeah, well, I'll add it to my list of New Year's resolutions."

Which I'll probably break in the first week.

"Now you're talking sense." She tosses the empty tray onto the floor with a clatter and starts on the next full one. It's the English scones. She picks one up and waves it at me. "And speaking of…when are you seeing your little English scone again? You need to make the most of it while he's here."

I shrug and swallow the pang of disappointment.

I haven't seen Alex in two days. Thirty-six hours. Since he left me on the floor. That sounds bad, but you know…he kind of did. That was Tuesday night—or rather, the early hours of Wednesday morning—and now it's Thursday morning. I thought he'd come in for cinnamon buns yesterday, but he didn't. Neither did his brothers.

He didn't drop the gingerbread house off, either, so perhaps he'll come in today.

Today is the deadline.

Or…the other option, something I've been trying not to think about, he's not bothering with the competition at all. Because now we've had sex—and he's got what he wanted—he doesn't need to bother.

He doesn't seem like the type of guy to do that, but on the other hand, *he's a guy.*

I keep reminding myself we didn't promise each other anything, we didn't make plans to see each other again. It doesn't matter that I quite possibly experienced the best night of my life. We had an unspoken deal. It was a one-time thing. Not to mention he's leaving Saturday.

And I *still* don't know his last name.

"We haven't made plans," I reply in a weird high pitch as I rip the tape off the top of the box. "Maybe he'll come by the bakery today. But whatever…I don't care."

Saylor pauses what she's doing—transferring Santa cookies onto the shelf—and lifts an eyebrow at me. Not sure why I thought I'd convince her; I'm not even convincing myself.

"I *don't* care," I mumble.

I don't. I mean, I do, because no one wants to be used for sex, even though I've done the exact same thing to him. But we all want to be wanted, including for, say…the next two days.

I peer over to the windows.

The line is long today, and nearly everyone has their hands full, carefully carrying their precious cargo of gingerbread houses. But Alex isn't there, nor are any of his brothers. I breathe through another pang of disappointment and shake it off.

"Okay. I'm going to open the doors." I swipe the keys from the counter. "Ready?"

"Yeah. Ready." Saylor picks up the stack of empty trays from the floor and takes them through to the kitchen, yelling, "Brock, we need you."

As predicted, today's the busiest morning of the week. Too busy.

We're so rushed off our feet I don't have time to think about Alex or my sore body. Everyone who's come in has also taken the opportunity to shop while they're here. We've been through four hundred cinnamon rolls and it's only eight thirty. Brock's still manning the till because, as usual, we couldn't cope.

We have a special drop-off point for the gingerbread houses, where six more bakery chefs take delivery, log the entry, and unbox them, before adding them onto the specially built display that runs along the side wall.

Right now, the houses are the first thing you see when you enter, and it looks so good. So

Christmassy, and even though I'm totally exhausted from working a gazillion jobs, and my body hurts in places I didn't know existed, seeing that shelf reminds me of how much I freaking *love* Christmas, and Aspen. My favorite houses aren't the fancy ones, like the Rivern Family, they're the ones with the little fingerprints swiped through the fondant icing on the roof.

Those are the ones that remind me of when I used to make them with my parents, or when Saylor and I would have decorating sessions together at each other's houses.

Thankfully, the morning counter rush is over by nine. Most people are out on the mountain, and everyone else likely saw the line in here and decided to come back later. Right now, it's quiet, and the rest of the morning will be a steady but manageable stream for Saylor and Brock, and I need to go and start my second job for the day before a line forms outside of there too.

"Hey, have you got this now? You mind if

I go?" I call to Saylor.

She shakes her head. "Go and sell some trees."

"I'll be back at lunchtime to help you clear up. Then we can head to Joe's for some food."

She waves me off. "Go."

I pour myself a big cup of coffee and skedaddle.

It's exactly fifty steps from the bakery to my store, so I know that I can always run back over if it's looking busy. I rush across the road, the thick rubber soles on my snow boots barely stopping me from slipping over. I've done it too many times to count but never seem to learn my lesson.

I can almost feel my parents waiting for me when I walk in and turn on all the lights. It's cooler than usual, and somehow that adds to the magic of this place. My mom liked it kept cold, because she said it was better for the wreaths and it was easier for us to wrap up warm. Plus, the door leading out to the tree pen was always open anyway, so it was totally pointless trying to heat it too much.

In here, I find the cold is comforting almost, and

every single time I walk in I stop for a minute, absorbing what my mom created—the rolls of paper, the overflowing boxes of multicolored ribbon and baubles, the decorations.

I love this place so much, and suddenly I'm not so tired. Because I remember why I'm busting my ass.

Because this place is slightly jumbled—the concrete floor is always covered in pine needles, and you normally come away covered in glitter no matter how still you stand—it never takes me very long to set up. Once I've unlocked the safe and filled up the till, I go and check on all the trees that will go out today from the preorder and delivery. Twisting my hair up into a knot, I pull my apron on and get to work.

Two more cups of coffee and a microwaved bowl of oatmeal later, and half of today's deliveries have already left, plus I've sold half a dozen more. It's been a busy morning with visitors popping in to buy gifts to take home, baubles for their trees, and Aspen regulars visiting to say hello, just like Mrs. Winslow.

She's been coming to this store since the day my mom opened it, and every year she buys her tree, two big wreaths for her doors, along with one decoration for each of her grandchildren to have for their trees.

"Oh Haven, these truly are so beautiful this year. Your mom and dad would be so proud of you. You always do them proud."

My cheeks heat, even in the cool air. "Thank you, Mrs. Winslow. I hope so."

"Oh, she would, she *would*," she coos, pulling a roll of notes from her purse and handing it to me to take what I need. She does this every time she shops here, and there's got to be a thousand dollars in fifties, so I peel a couple off and hand her back the rest. "Where are you spending Christmas Day, dear? Not in the house on your own?"

I shake my head with a smile. "No, I'll be at Saylor's, like every year."

"Good, don't want you rattling about up there

by yourself." She pats my hand. "Don't forget our place is always open."

"No, ma'am. Don't you worry, Saylor and I will be together." I smile as the shop bell rings, alerting me to a new customer. "Thank you, though."

I pick up the wreath to carry out, but my eyes land on who's walked through the door. My heart skips around like a schoolgirl as Alex holds my gaze. He nods over to the side of the store and steps toward the baubles, leaving me to finish helping Mrs. Winslow.

"Let's get this to the car."

It takes me a couple of minutes to help her down the store steps and place the wreath in her trunk. Because I also have to say hi to Mr. Winslow, who's been patiently waiting for her on the curb, Alex has been in the store alone for five minutes. He doesn't turn when the bell rings; he's staring at the photo of my parents and me that sits on a shelf behind the counter. It was taken the same day as the one Joe has on the wall in The Old Saloon, when we were out planting saplings.

I close the door behind me. I'm tempted to switch the Open sign to Closed, but I don't.

"Hey."

"Hey." Alex spins, pushing his hands into his pockets.

He's so goddamn handsome with his thick stubble and hair all messy. Today there's this intensely rugged quality about him, like he's just returned from a week of rock climbing or something, and now I could totally imagine him throwing hay bales, or wrangling cows. He stands there with a smile that's making me wonder if he's also thinking about all the things we did together, but his cheeks aren't going red like *I know* mine are.

He points behind him at the picture. "Are these your parents?"

I glance past his shoulder and nod. "Yeah, Wyatt and Jeanne Wylder. And that's me in the middle."

His gaze flicks back to the photo. "You're

cute."

"Thank you." I smile, biting down on my lip so I'm not smiling too much and make it weird. "So…did you come for more decorations?"

He shakes his head. "No. I came to tell you that I've handed my gingerbread house in."

My eyes widen in surprise. "Really?"

"Yeah. I meant to come earlier, but it wasn't ready. Your friend told me you were over here, so I came to see you." His smile grows and a warm, fuzzy feeling slips across my skin.

"Oh, well, I'll go and check it out."

We stand there staring at each other. It's exactly the same as the first time, with this weird magnetism between us, the air thickening with tension and unspoken words. Except now I don't have to imagine what he looks like naked, because *I know*. I know what he's capable of doing with his tongue. I know how it feels when he's inside me.

Mind blowing.

His eyes flick toward the door, and he steps closer to me. "I have to go and meet my brothers, but I'll come and find you later to collect my prize."

"Your prize?"

"For winning."

My head falls back with a laugh. "I've never met anyone as cocky as you."

"Confident," he corrects me with a wink, leaning in to kiss my cheek, and I'm enveloped once more with the scent of oak and leather.

Turning to smile before he jogs down the steps, I watch from the window until he's hopped into a Range Rover parked on the street and taken off. The second he disappears around the block, I twist the sign to Closed and sprint across the road. As fast as my snow boots will allow, of course.

It's almost like Saylor is waiting for me. "Oh man, Havey. Your English crumpet has it baaad."

"What?"

"No one cares about a gingerbread competition

this much. No one. Not even the Riverns. He's into you *big time*." Saylor jerks her head toward the shelves. "You'll see."

I stand and stare, trying to figure out what I'm supposed to be looking at when I see it.

Right in the middle.

My heart thuds hard in my chest. I'm tempted to rub my eyes in case I'm seeing things. I definitely blink.

But it's still there when I open them.

My store. My store in *gingerbread.*

My store in precise detail.

The Wylder Trees sign swings over the door, even the bell outside the shop is there, and the wreaths on the windows. All made of gingerbread. Around to the side, the trees organized by height in the pen. The little bench Alex sat on. The archway with the mistletoe. Everything is there.

Inside, the shop is laid out just so. The shelves filled with tree ornaments. The counter where I serve my customers. The drawers overflowing with ribbons and baubles.

I don't even know how he's done it. How he pulled this together so quickly—where did he get the doll's house furniture from?

I've never seen anything like it.

Then I notice the envelope with my name on it resting against the side, and I rip it open. There are five words on the card I pull out.

Told you I'd win…

Alex x

Alexander

12

"TO THE LEFT, MILO. LEFT. LEFT," Hendricks yells, hands cupped around his mouth for a makeshift megaphone. "LEFT FOR FUCK'S SAKE."

He's too far over the field to hear, but let's call it that twin thing, because Miles spins his pony, leans so far out of his saddle he's defying gravity, and smacks the ball perfectly between the goalposts.

The crowds go wild; Aspen glitterati cheering, whistling, and, like Lando, sloshing their drinks everywhere as their hands shoot up in the air.

Miles's team—distinguishable in their navy shirts with pale blue numbers stitched onto the back—has taken the lead at the end of the second chukka, thanks to our baby brother. The umpire's flag goes up, and the ponies thunder back down the snow-covered field to where their grooms are waiting to lead them off.

"How the fuck did he make that shot?" Lando marvels, with a shake of his head and a broad grin. It's a grin like the Lando of old, pre-Caroline.

Neither Hendricks nor I answer because it's a rhetorical question, the same one we ask every time we watch Miles play.

He has this innate ability to get a pony to do whatever he asks of them in situations that seem impossible to anyone else. While all four of us have ridden since we could walk, Miles is the one with the talent inherited from our father.

He would have loved to watch him.

"I'm going to the bar before the next chukka. Same again?" Lando asks but walks off without waiting for a response.

Hendricks lifts a beer bottle to his lips and drains it. "At least we know where Max gets it from."

Ah yes, Maxwell Burlington—next generation's future England polo player.

"How *is* my favorite nephew?" I turn and ask. "Enjoying some time with Granny and Auntie Clementine?"

He rolls his eyes, and his cheeks puff with a dry chuckle.

While Hendricks has a full-time nanny to help with Max, our mother also likes to spend as much time with him as possible, and she's wrapped around his finger. It's something we're all aware of, including my three-year-old nephew. Therefore, it's highly likely we'll return to a child hopped up on sugar who's had far too many late nights.

"*Granny* took him to meet Father Christmas yesterday. I swear I'll get back to Burlington and my son will have put in a parent transfer request or whatever. He's three, and he already thinks I'm boring as fuck." He laughs dryly. "Boring father. Absent mother. Poor kid."

Max is a result of a brief romance Hendricks had with a girl he met one night in London. It wasn't anything serious, and they'd hook up whenever he was in the city. A couple of months in, she told him she was pregnant, and she was keeping the baby. Once the initial shock wore off, Hendricks, in his typical unruffled fashion, took his impending fatherhood in his stride—supporting Sienna—Max's mother—as best he could, attending all the pre-baby meetings with doctors and choosing hospitals, and whatever else goes on when you're about to have a baby.

I wouldn't know.

However, when Max was six months old, Hendricks came over to my house in what could only be described as an emotional state. Miles was in Argentina playing polo, and I'm the next rung on the ladder for problem solving.

Since they'd discovered Sienna was pregnant, Hendricks had been trying to make a relationship with her work. He reduced his hours at his clinic to spend more time in London, but even during her pregnancy it became clear that the longer he spent with her, the less he liked her. It didn't help that Hendricks is a country boy through and through. His days comprise of healing sick animals, whereas Sienna seemed to be allergic to being out of London in a way that no amount of antihistamine could help.

But then Max arrived; this blue-eyed, dark-haired baby boy, and we all fell in love with him.

Everyone, except Sienna.

Sienna still wanted to go out and party. She wanted to party with Hendricks's money, while Hendricks stayed home and looked after their newborn son. Which he did. To say it caused strain in their relationship is an understatement. He wanted her to have her life—he hired help, he gave her everything she needed to feel like she *had* her life—but Max still needed to be the priority, and it was clear he wasn't.

The last straw was when she disappeared to Ibiza for two weeks with some friends. Hendricks had gone back to Valentine Nook for the day to help deliver a foal, and Sienna told the nanny to drop Max off at Burlington.

It didn't take long for the judge to award Hendricks full custody. In the eighteen months since Max has lived at Burlington with us, Sienna's seen him six times. Usually when she wants more money. Hendricks barely left his side while Max settled into his new stability. He's the sweetest, kindest little boy, usually found covered in mud and with a dog or two following him somewhere. Max loves his life—he doesn't really know any different—but I know Hendricks carries a huge amount of guilt for *choosing the wrong woman,* as he often puts it, and denying Max the opportunity for two parents.

But I don't know anyone who's a better father than my brother.

"You are pretty boring, Henners." I ruffle his head with a laugh. "Especially compared to Granny and Auntie Clementine."

"Yeah, I know." He grins. "But I guess my son will have to deal with it. At least until he's eighteen."

I pick up my beer and sip. "He will."

"This week is the longest I've ever been away from him, you know," he adds quietly.

"Is it?"

"Yes."

"Ready to go home?"

"Absolutely." He grins wide. "But, I'm glad we came, even if it was under these particular circumstances. I think we all needed this break together."

I nod in agreement. The pair of us are looking out on the polo field, but I can tell Hendricks is side-eyeing me.

"Are you ready to go home? Or not wanting to leave a certain tree seller quite yet?"

I pause before shrugging, as I think about my answer.

"Because…I know it's hard for you, Al. Christmas. It's hard for all of us. We all miss him, we just chose to do it differently. But the past few days, you've seemed more relaxed than usual…" He goes quiet. "I thought maybe it was because we've all been swept up in the Lando and Caroline drama."

My answer is, I'm ready to go home. The anniversary of my father's death is next week, and it always brings an added edge of anxiety to December for me on top of all the Christmas stuff. And on that day, I like to be back home at Burlington, with my family.

But Hendricks is right, we *have* all been swept up in the Lando and Caroline drama, which could be the reason why I haven't been quite so bothered about the Christmassy-ness of this week.

Except it's not.

And it's not because I was with my brothers—just the four of us together for the first time in a long time.

It's Haven.

There's something about this girl. This insanely hot girl, with her insanely hot body—both hard and soft in all the right places. The girl I may possibly have had the best night of sex in my life with, her Christmas nails wrapped around my dick.

I enjoy her company. I like hearing her laugh. I like *making* her laugh.

And bizarrely, it's the Christmas thing. *Yeah, I know.*

I like her love of all things Christmas, because her parents loved it. Her parents died and they loved Christmas, so she loves Christmas.

My dad died, and it killed any love I had for Christmas.

The irony.

I can't stop thinking about it. It's why I left her that night, it's why I didn't go to the bakery yesterday. It's why I made her store out of gingerbread.

It had been one of those lightbulb moments

where you can't quite pinpoint exactly where it came from.

Lando, Hendricks, and I had been aimlessly sticking pieces of gingerbread together, trying to decide what to make. Miles had mostly been breaking off chunks and dunking it into his coffee, while banging on about what great work we'd done with decorating the tree we bought. Hendricks was telling us how Max had been playing with Auntie Clementine's old dolls' house, but complaining about how there weren't any Christmas trees in it.

What if we made Haven's tree shop? I had suggested.

I'd ordered a rush delivery on Amazon, and all the dolls' house furniture I could find arrived the next morning. I'm still undecided whether it was a totally over-the-top stupid idea.

"Did you see Haven when you dropped the house off?"

I nod. "Yeah, she was in her shop, so I went and told her."

I can still feel the insane electricity between us, the second it sparked after she looked up and saw me standing there. My dick can feel it too.

"Did we earn first place?" He grins.

"I'm quietly confident we have." I laugh. "I know you didn't sign up to make gingerbread, but it was a fun day. I owe you big time for helping. Always useful having someone who can cook."

He turns to me with knitted brows. "Al, we didn't cook anything."

"Yeah, but you know what I mean. You helped with all the icing and shit. And cutting the shapes. That's cooking in my book."

"It's literally the opposite of cooking." He shakes his head. "Are you seeing her again?"

I shrug. "Maybe."

I don't want to admit how much I want to, because I *really* want to.

It's been a while since I've had a night like that. Not sure I've *ever* had a night like that.

Uninhibited fucking, brought on by an attraction I've never experienced.

"Running out of time."

I nod. "Yeah, I know."

"We don't have plans tonight. Go and see her, Al. Have some fun."

"Milo will have plans for us after he wins this match." I laugh, as the ponies all charge back out onto the snow. I turn around in my seat. "Where's Lan?"

"There." Hendricks glances over in the direction of the bar and nods to Lando, who's carrying three bottles of beer and pushing through the densely packed crowds.

"It's a bloody scrum in there," he grumbles, sitting down in his vacant seat. "Worse than Twickenham."

"Told you we should have sat in the seats Miles left for us."

"They're too far away. I like to be next to the action." Lando passes a bottle each to Hendricks and me as one of Miles's teammates gallops down the edge of the field, so close to us that I feel the wind in my face.

"You won't like it if you get smacked in the head by a flying ball."

He lifts his bottle to his lips. "If that happens, I'll just pull you in front of me as a shield. The ball can hit you instead."

"Touché."

"Hey, who's that guy over there?" Lando nods toward the stands farther down the field, where a guy dressed head to toe in black is walking in our direction. He's surrounded by women—short, tall, blonde, brunette, redhead—all working to keep up with his long strides. "He looks familiar."

The three of us watch as the guy passes in front of us, eyes straight ahead. He's almost menacingly still, completely ignoring anyone around him, while they all part like the Red Sea to let him pass. Two-thirds of the way down the field, a Rolls-Royce SUV pulls up between the spectator stands, where the guy swaps out with the driver, and leaves.

"Santiago Torres," replies Hendricks, his tone dripping in scorn and disapproval. "The Argentinian number three."

"Him? That's the guy Milo got in a fight with last year when he nearly got trampled on?"

"The very same."

"What's he doing here? I thought he was banned from polo for two years."

Hendricks shrugs. "He was. Is."

"Does Miles know?"

Hendricks shrugs again. "He wasn't here yesterday, he would have mentioned it."

"Bloody hell, he won't be pleased," I reply, just as Miles scores another goal and the crowd once more whoops and hollers. "Shit, need to pay attention to this. Miles will definitely quiz us on 'what we feel were his best moments of his game.'"

"Definitely that second goal," adds Lando.

Miles's team wins four goals to two.

As predicted, the party starts immediately after. Champagne is freely poured into anyone's empty glass. Burgers and fried chicken are offered around on platters. Polo fans are everywhere. Miles disappears with a girl. The evening draws in and nighttime descends like a set of blackout blinds. Fire pits are lit, industrial heaters are turned on, and a plethora of blankets are handed out.

I spend most of the next few hours with Lando and Hendricks, my mind drifting back to Haven every couple of minutes, wondering what she's doing and where she is. I ruminate on whether to go and find her or leave our night for what it was. One night of glorious fucking.

Because what's the point in going back for more when I leave in two days?

But the pull of seeing her again becomes too strong, and I find myself calling a driver to take me up to her house.

I don't have her phone number, I don't even know if she's there.

I second-guess myself for the entire journey until I knock on the front door, and know that coming here was possibly the best decision of my life to date.

She answers wearing sleep shorts, a thick pair of woolly socks, and a hoodie with Wylder Ranch on the front, along with a smile and green eyes as wide as dinner plates. Her hair is loose, tumbling down her shoulders, and all I want to do is wrap it around my fist.

"I'm here to bribe the judge," I manage to say before she tugs on the front of my jacket, pulling me into the house, and my lips crash to hers.

Haven

13

"Yeah, right there. Oh *god*…your dick…"

"Was made for your pussy," Alex groans, his voice taut as his mouth seals around my nipple while he slowly thrusts inside me.

I can tell this dick is ruining me. Has ruined me already.

How am I going to manage once he leaves for England?

"Yeah, fuck…oh my god."

It's been like this since he knocked on my door, god knows how long ago. A couple of orgasms at least.

There I was, minding my own business, on my way to bed, and trying not to think about Alex or what he meant when he said he'd come and find me later. Because it was getting pretty goddamn late. Late enough I'd already set my vibrator up on charge.

And then there was a bang on the door, and my night greatly improved.

"Hold it, Haven. You're not fucking coming until I say so," he grits out. "You've already had three, you can wait this time."

Oh yeah…he arrived three orgasms ago.

I don't want to wait, so I take no notice and roll my hips in his lap. His fingers are digging into my thighs so hard they'll leave marks on top of the marks fading from the other night. Reminders of what we did when he's back in England.

"Haven…greedy girl," he warns.

I am greedy. I don't even know how I managed to wait the two days since Alex was last here. He's woken a monster in me, and I need more.

"Alex, please. I need it."

"You need my cock?"

"Hmmm…yes."

"Say it."

"I need your cock."

He grips my thighs, holding me still while he drives into me with such force it steals the air from my lungs.

"Like that? Need it *like that*?"

"Ahhhh."

"Words, Haven, use your words."

"Yes, Alex, god, yeees. I need it like that… *fuck*…your dick…" My eyes have full on rolled into my head.

"Fuck my dick?" He chuckles. "You certainly are."

He slaps his hands on my ass cheeks, one on either side, and grips onto them, his fingers kneading my crack, and I don't think I've ever felt anything quite so good. Not while his magical dick is slamming so deep inside me I know it's branded me. I will never belong to anything except Alex's dick.

It's been like this for hours; relentless, punishing, delicious.

I'm whimpering, beads of sweat drip down the column of my throat, my thighs clenched hard to stop the shuddering. My entire body is as tight and strained as a stretched rubber band. One tiny flick, and it will snap in half. I'm trying to hold on, but it's like stopping an eighteen-wheeler hurtling right toward you.

Alex is still grasping onto a semblance of control, his hand gripping the back of my neck, but I can tell from the way his jaw slackens and his eyes glaze, navy and hooded, that he's close.

I've seen him come so many times now that *I can tell.*

And holy shit, but he's even more beautiful.

My orgasm hits almost with no warning, a sucker punch. All I can get out is a garbled "Al…" before I detonate around him, nails scraping along his back for some kind of leverage, no doubt leaving thick welts in his skin. But I need something to stop me falling into this oblivion he's pushed me into, almost painfully.

Alex explodes inside me.

Even through the tiny membrane of latex he's wearing, I can feel the force of him coming. We collapse onto each other, gasping for air though there's none, and all we're doing is sucking down carbon dioxide. My body is mush; I've flopped into the most uncomfortable position, but I don't have a shred of energy left in me to move, or care.

"The boys are going to have to take my body back to England with them. I'm dead." Alex grunts into my chest, the tickle of his stubble slipping through my sweat.

"We'll need to be buried together," I puff out. "I'm dead too."

He laughs as best he can, seeing as we're both still catching our breath. "Best way to go, I say. And I nearly didn't come over."

I turn my head to face him. "Why?"

"Wasn't sure you'd be here. And if you were here, I didn't want to be presumptuous about how much you like my dick."

"I think we can safely presume I'm more than happy you and your dick are here." I rearrange myself to flop my head back onto the pillow, though sadly, it breaks the connection between Alex and me, and his dick slips away, leaving nothing but cool air between my legs. "Even if you have killed us both."

"Hey, you killed me first."

I raise an eyebrow. "Yeah?"

"Definitely."

I watch as he peels off the condom, ties it, and deposits it in the bathroom trash with the rest. I'm waiting to see if this time is the time he decides to get dressed and head back to the cabin where his brothers are, but he slides silently back in next to me instead.

Opening my mouth to say something, my tongue has other ideas and sticks to the roof. Seems all that kissing—and sex—has left my mouth in desperate need of hydration. In fact, given the amount we've both sweated through the last few hours, I think we could probably do with electrolytes too.

"Water?"

He nods. "Good idea."

I don't bother to get dressed to go downstairs. It might be freezing outside, but I'm still boiling hot. Grabbing a couple of glasses from the cabinet, I fill them with ice and top them up with water, and when I turn around to go back upstairs, I'm not alone.

I was drunk the other night, but now I can truly appreciate Alex in all my sober glory.

He leans against the door frame and I take him in; thick, sculpted thighs, broad chest from years of workouts. He's not just athletic, he's strong, dedicated. Biceps powerful enough to carry my weight while I'm pinned against the door and he's driving into me.

Once again I realize my mistake when I thought Alex didn't look like he was the type of guy who worked in farming, but now he's standing in front of me, I can't do anything *but* imagine him honing his muscles hauling logs, or controlling a stallion with a squeeze of his thick thighs.

But it's the trimmed, soft, dark hair running along the deep line below his hips that draws my gaze. *That,* and his dick standing to attention, because it doesn't seem to have an off switch.

He's watching me. And I'm heating up all over again, burning under the intensity of his stare.

I swallow.

He's waiting to see what I'm going to do, and I remember what he said to me the other night. Taking a sip of water, I hold an ice cube in my mouth and sink to my knees.

Alex is statue still.

Only the shallow rise and fall of his chest, and the throbbing of his jutting dick, hard and proud, as he watches me are any indication he's real life and not made of marble.

He winces as my cold tongue licks up the

bead of precum forming on the end, before I shift the cube over and run it along the length of his cock. Alex's hand shoots out and grips the kitchen counter as he mumbles a string of curse words I can't quite decipher, but it's *hot*. The power I'm currently wielding, that I can bring this man to his knees with my mouth.

Wrapping my hand around the base of his shaft, I take the head of his dick between my lips, swirling my tongue over the slit. A groan rumbles out of him.

"Haven, this feels…*fuck*—incredible. Your mouth. You look un*real. Absolutely unreal.*"

I glance up to find him watching me, and he holds my gaze as I work the rest of him into my mouth alongside the ice cube. And it's *work.* I'm trying not to choke, my mouth spread wide open, but the reaction on Alex's face makes it totally worth it. The hot and cold contrast has his brain work overtime.

I pause and pull back off with a pop, then resume my position, dropping my hand so I can take him deeper. His entire body clenches when I moan, the vibrations from my throat forcing his eyes shut as he concentrates on every sensation I'm waving over him, and my eyes close too.

"Incredible…" he mumbles again from above as he drags his thumb over my bottom lip and cups my cheek before I realize what he's doing. His thumb pulls my mouth open further, until the ice cube is forced across my tongue. "Enough of that." The ice cube clatters in the sink where he tossed it, before he guides himself back. "If you're going to choke, it'll be on my dick and nothing else."

There's so much room in my mouth now, and I roll my tongue along the underside of his dick before drawing him back out so I can take him deeper.

His hand slips around to the base of my neck, something I've always *hated,* but with Alex, it spurs me on. I want it to be good for him. Each time my head bobs, I feel it between my thighs, dripping out of me, as I take him further, until my nose is brushing against his soft hair.

"Jesus—" he groans, though there's an underlying tone to it. *Awe.* "You're so good at this."

His balls are tightening in my hands, his dick is throbbing. He's so close, and one hard suck is all it takes for him to spill down my throat with a garbled cry, slashing the air with a string of expletives.

He buckles forward while also protecting me from being crushed, his pelvis juddering as I keep sucking, and swallow him down.

"Dreams really do come true." He pulls me up by my arm, twisting me around so quickly I would have fallen if he hadn't been holding me.

My back is to his chest, until it isn't. Until I'm bent ninety degrees over the kitchen table. My tits squash and my palms are forced flat onto the cool, wooden surface, with my burning face resting on top.

"Don't move," he growls, kneeling behind me.

Spreading my cheeks, his tongue drags between them, lapping me up. And oh *god*…

"You loved my cock in your mouth, didn't you, Haven? I can see right here."

I cry out as his tongue spears inside me.

"You're a mess. Such a messy girl, that I need to clean."

His finger slips down to my sensitive, pulsing clit, but instead of giving me the exact amount of pressure he knows I need. He stills.

He stands up. His dick thickens as he bends over me, his breath hot against my ear, "Tell me how much you want this."

All I can do is whimper, but I know I'm not getting anything until I tell him. Especially when he removes his hand entirely.

"That first day I saw you next to the jukebox, I knew I wanted to fuck you. But I never thought I'd enjoy fucking you *this much*. I never want this to end."

There's a pause. I don't think either of us are breathing.

Was that too much? Too honest?

I mean, I'm not going to see him again after Saturday, so what does it matter? But still…telling a guy I never want him to stop fucking me might be a *little* extreme.

But then he chuckles. "Good girl."

After that, it's like he's on a mission. His tongue and fingers relentlessly working to bring me another orgasm. I don't know how he does it, but every time, it's like I've been so starved for months that I'm desperate for more, and I can't hold out.

His fingers trace up and down the ridges of my spine. It's relaxing, *too* relaxing. Maybe this table would be a suitable place to fall asleep.

I'm drifting off when Alex's deep voice pulls me back to the present.

"I think we should get in that shower of yours, clean up."

I blink as I register what he's saying. "You're staying?"

"I'm staying," he replies in a way that doesn't invite argument. "And we're making the most of it."

Oh god. I don't know if I *can* make the most of it. My body is screaming for more sex, while my brain is begging me for sleep. Somewhere down the line I stifle a yawn, which he catches, and slaps my ass.

I'm wide awake now.

"You can sleep tomorrow, Haven."

"I *can't,*" I wail. "Tomorrow is the gingerbread house judging. It takes all day."

"Another reason to name me the winner." He smirks. "It'll save you time. Now get in that shower."

Alexander

14

For the second time this week I wake up with absolutely no idea of where I am.

Today, thank god, the hangover is missing, so it takes me much less time than before to figure it out.

Haven. I'm at Haven's.

Shifting onto my side, I turn my head and there's nothing but an empty expanse of sheets and a thick, bunched-up comforter, when I'd prefer there to be a person.

Haven, to be precise.

There's also intense silence.

No sound of footsteps, no shower

running or tap dripping. The scent of fresh morning coffee is missing.

I ease up to sitting, my eyes darting around the room until they land on something that puts an instant frown on my face. My clothes, folded and placed on the ottoman in the corner.

"Haven?" I call, though I already know there's going to be no answer.

She's not here, and somehow I've slept through a girl leaving me in her bed.

This is *new*.

Even from the various women I've dated over the years, including Grace, my most recent ex, I've never been in their house while they weren't there. I've never been left in bed. Never not woken up.

Usually when sleepovers happen, they're at my place, because I'm a creature of habit. I like my things. My bed. My space.

Being in someone else's bed without them? I didn't think I'd like that.

It's too intimate. Too familiar.

And yet, lying here, on a mattress that could be made of clouds based on how comfortable it is, I could quite easily fall back to sleep for the rest of the day.

I don't get that opportunity however, as a buzzing cuts through the silence. I realize it's my phone, which I find in the pocket of my jeans and only just manage to answer with a grunt before it rings out.

"Al, where the fuck are you?"

I recover from the daze I'm in at the speed with which I hurled myself out of bed, and scrub a hand down my face.

"I'm at Haven's," I tell Miles and ignore the sly chuckle he lets out.

"Interesting. I'm calling to let you know it's ten a.m. and today's the last day for hitting the slopes. How much longer do you need to say goodbye?" he adds with a snort.

I glance around the room, peer my head out of the bedroom door. Yup. I'm definitely in the house by myself.

"I'm ready."

"Excellent. Lando's just emerged, so we'll leave in an hour."

"Cool," I reply, though an hour is wildly optimistic, seeing as I still need to wake up properly, get dressed, and Haven's place is right across town. I catch him just before he hangs up, and blurt, "Milo, can you come and get me, please?"

I take his loud laughter as confirmation, hang up, and send him a pin drop.

Reaching for my clothes, I debate jumping into the shower for a lightning wash but then decide I can shower back at the house. It was only around three a.m. when I finished cleaning Haven up in the bathtub, so I'm probably not smelling as disgusting as I would be otherwise. And I kind of like the scent of her still on me.

We leave tomorrow and I won't get another chance to experience it. The thought of which twists my gut.

I'm still trying not to think about leaving as

I get dressed and head downstairs, before stopping halfway for a little chuckle to myself. Haven might not have woken me up, or even made any coffee, but she's had time to turn on every single Christmas light and dancing ornament.

I was totally right when I said I expected her house to be covered in Christmas trees. There are trees and decorations everywhere. Glittery objects on every shelf. Way more than I noticed the last time I was here, even last night, though admittedly I was far too distracted by Haven's tits and mouth, and the way her arse fitted perfectly in my hands, to pay attention to anything else.

On my way into the kitchen, I spy a wall of framed photos and stop in front of it. Haven stares back at me in all stages of her life—a bouncing baby on her mother's knee, wobbling on skis, riding horses. I spot a couple similar to the one she's hung in the store. These are not just photos, it's a wall of memories, like one we have at Burlington—

all five of us as children, Max, the animals, our parents.

Just like ours doesn't feature our father beyond me as a young teenager, there are no pictures of Haven's parents with her as a fully-fledged adult. I wonder how often she stands in front of this wall and dreams about what life would be like if they were still here.

Is it as often as I do at home?

We might live seven thousand miles apart, but grief doesn't discriminate. I find myself thinking how lucky I am to still have the rest of my family, when Haven has been left to fend by herself.

I can't imagine what I would have done, if I'd been left to run our family business by myself.

Fuck it up for sure.

The volume of decisions alone I'd have to make would fry my brain, and that's without all the labor on top. Lando and I make a good team, throw in the dozens of farmhands and management team we have on top, and we can cope—and that's only talking about those directly involved with the running of the Burlington Estate and Valentine Nook.

Add in the rest of the businesses we have around the world, and we're talking nearly ten thousand employees.

I know Haven's business isn't the same size, but something tells me it's almost more pressure. I've never met anyone who works as much as she does, including Lando, who would quite easily run himself into the ground if left to his own devices. But the hours I've seen her working this week makes me think it's not solely about how much she loves Christmas trees.

A sudden burst of sunlight stops me from pondering on it any more, pulling my attention toward the kitchen. It certainly looks different in the daylight, and I allow myself a smile as the memory of Haven bent over the table hurtles back into my brain. I'm certain I'll never experience sex like that again.

My dick's been ruined by an American Christmas Tree farmer. Go figure.

I debate making a coffee, but it's already been twenty minutes since I hung up on Miles, and knowing my luck, he'll arrive the second I switch the machine on, and I kind of want to leave this place exactly as I found it. Like I was never here.

Because, irrationally, I think that if I leave no trace, if I don't familiarize myself with anything else in this house beyond what I already know, then it'll be easier to forget about her and move on when I return to England. Forget about the way it felt to be inside her, the tight warmth of her pussy clenching my dick, watching her teeth sink into her lip as she tried to hold onto her orgasm. Or the way my name rolled off her tongue – deep and breathy – when she no longer could.

It's not going to do me any good to remember.

With that in mind, I creep out of the front door and close it behind me.

The sun is so bright it's taking away the chill in the air. Dropping down onto the porch step next to one of the nutcrackers (eye roll), I take in the view.

It's even more impressive than the one at Murray's place, and maybe this view actually *is* the sole reason Haven works so hard. I can truly understand why. Over the valley from our cabin, the mountains on this side seem so much bigger. There's a never-ending forest of trees, and I imagine Haven out here in all seasons with her crew planting, logging, and prepping.

For the briefest of seconds, I wonder what she could accomplish here if she had the resources we have at Burlington, but it's gone the moment I hear the crunch of car tires on gravel, and the Range Rover comes into sight.

Miles pulls up to the front steps and lowers his window.

"Good morning, Alexander." He peers over to the Father Christmas and reindeer, followed by the nutcrackers. "Well don't you look like the prettiest Christmas picture sitting there. Want me to take your photo?"

"I do not," I grumble as I round the car and hop into the passenger side. "But thanks for coming to get me."

"You're welcome. I brought you a coffee." He nods at the to-go cup in the cup holder, the scent of which already has saliva pooling in my mouth.

"My hero." I ease it out and take a long sip. "Thanks."

"Again, you're welcome."

I turn to Miles, we're still sitting in the car and he's staring at me with a broad smile stretching from ear to ear.

"What?"

He shakes his head. "Nothing. I just love being right."

"What exactly are you right about?"

"You getting laid. You look thoroughly fu—"

I roll my eyes. "Just drive, Milo."

Haven

15

"Haven, dear…Haven? HAVEN."

I spin around at the tap on my shoulder to find Mr. Roundtree, from the Aspen General Store across the road, looking agitated, and apologetic. But mostly agitated. I lower my hands covering my ears.

"Hey, Mr. Roundtree!" I shout, pretending like I don't know why he's come in. But I know. "What's up?"

"Do you think you can do something about that?" He jabs his finger to where the band is warming up.

It's the Christmas band

Mrs. Loughty booked before she left for her round-the-world trip—and more evidence that she wanted to turn her back on the entire holiday season.

The band is *so loud.* And awful. Really awful.

I think they're playing "Santa Baby," but I'm not sure. Sounds like a couple of cats being strangled.

They've only been going half an hour, and it's truly a miracle Mr. Roundtree is the first person to come in and complain.

I sigh. "I'm so sorry, Mr. Roundtree. Let me deal with it."

"Thank you, dear. I know you're working hard for today, but I've not had any customers this morning."

"Don't worry, it'll be okay." I pat him on the shoulder and walk over to where Saylor is carefully arranging the gingerbread houses. "Say, I'm going to get the music turned down."

She looks up at me and pulls the balled-up cotton wool from her ears. "What?"

I roll my eyes, because why didn't I think of that. "Shall we ask them to turn the music down?"

"Oh god, *yes.* No one's going to come if this is what they're greeted with. It's loud enough to start an avalanche."

"Yeah." I nod and follow Mr. Roundtree outside.

I didn't realize how much the windows had been muffling the sound, because the moment I open the doors I swear my eardrums burst. Mr. Roundtree hurries off to safety, while I stand in front of the makeshift stage that is erected for the band and competition presentation every year.

It's super hard to get their attention—all five of them rocking out to whatever it is they're playing—*hell if I know*—all five of them with their eyes shut. In the end, I spy the adaptor cords plugged into the amplifiers and yank it out.

My bones immediately stop vibrating

from the bass and there's silence. Sweet, sweet silence.

"Cut!" the lead singer shouts to his bandmates, glancing around to figure out the source of his broken speakers, before his beady eyes narrow on me holding two ends of a plug—one in each hand. "Is there a problem?"

"Yeah, we need the volume lowered. We can't hear ourselves speak in the store."

He swipes his long bangs away from his eyes and peers down from the elevated platform he's standing on, squinting through the windows.

"There's no one in there."

"That's true." I nod. "Very true. But there will be, and when they are, we're going to need to hear what they're saying. So can we keep the volume down?"

He says nothing, so I cross my arms and find myself in a stare off with the guy. I'm certain none of them are old enough to drink, and I'm hoping if I stand here long enough he'll find me suitably intimidating. I'm tired and antsy today, and certainly not in the mood to be messed with.

"Sure, but you're not going to get the full effect of our creative output," he huffs, eventually.

"It's 'Jingle Bells,' bud. We can manage." I turn back to the store. "Thanks."

"Nice work, Havey." Saylor slow claps when I'm in the warmth again, with the door closed. "Well handled."

Her mouth is twitching, I know she's holding onto a laugh because she rarely sees me snappy. Or in a bad mood. Not that I'm in a bad mood *per se* but I'm not in a *great* mood.

Normally she's the bad guy of the two of us. She's the one used to dealing with unruly kids.

"What?"

"Nothing, I just sometimes forget what you're like when you're moody."

"Ugh. I'll take them some cinnamon buns, they'll be fine."

"Haven, the whole street will thank you

for getting rid of that terrible noise." She frowns, sweeping her arm over to the doors. "Plus, they've not stopped playing. They're still terrible, just quieter. I don't know what Mrs. Loughty was thinking, they're not the usual guys she has."

I shrug, because I've been thinking the same.

For the gingerbread competition finale, there's usually a very jolly Christmassy band outside the store, occasionally one of the groups Joe books in The Old Saloon, and they all dress up in Santa costumes, which the kids love. The main road is cordoned off to traffic, so everyone stays around, hanging in the street drinking hot chocolate, queuing up for food trucks stationed at the far end, or eating whatever they've bought from the store. The whole town gets involved, and everyone loves it.

But the guys who turned up this morning look like they'd be more at home in a high schooler's garage with posters of Metallica. There's nothing remotely Christmassy about them, and thinking about it, they did seem super surprised holiday tunes were on the playlist for today.

"Yeah, I dunno. But at least we can hear ourselves think now." I switch on the coffee machine, because I *need* coffee. "What do we have left to do?"

The pair of us look up as a loud clatter comes from the direction of the kitchens, and Kyle starts shouting. This morning has been a little high stress, to put it bluntly.

The Saturday finale is the one day of the year when the bakery opens later—ten a.m. and stays open until after the winners are announced later in the afternoon. But no matter how much later the doors are opening today, there still doesn't seem to be enough time to get everything done.

Yesterday, Saylor, Kyle, and I, plus a couple of the local Aspen celebrities spent the day judging the two thousand entries. I've never been part of the judging as I've always entered, so I hadn't realized quite how tricky it was, or how much work it entailed.

The houses were sorted into categories—Traditional, Under 10s, Most Creative…etc.—

then each category has a winner, runner-up, and third place, and once they've all been decided, a Best in Show is chosen. It took *all day.*

This year's entries are strong. The Rivern family's, another group who turned their house into a cable car with skiers inside, and a super-traditional European-style house with lots of piped icing. Surprisingly, only one Santa's Workshop this year, complete with Candy Cane Lane.

But I only have eyes for Alex's.

Several times I zoned out because I was staring at its little swinging Wylder Trees sign outside. Or the tiny bell. The door with its panes set out in frosting. I still don't know how he managed to make it quite so beautiful and detailed. It's the most precious gingerbread house I've ever seen. All the more so because it was made for me.

It is impossible not to be biased either. Because in my opinion it should easily win every category, except Under 10s.

The race to win is close, but more importantly,

we've raised nearly seventy thousand dollars this year, and a check will be presented to the local children's hospital after the winners are announced at the presentation this afternoon."

I glance over to Saylor when I realize she's talking, because I zoned out again. "Huh?"

"There are still some houses to move out from the kitchens to the display. The winning entries are front and center already." She gently taps the swinging sign on Alex's house—winner of *The Most Creative Gingerbread House.* "Are we expecting our new champion to come in and collect his prize?"

Sucking in my cheek, I shrug a shoulder. I'm not sure. "He's going home today. I don't know what time his flight is."

She walks over and throws her arm around me, which weirdly makes me want to cry. "Don't worry, Havey. He'll come, I'm sure. He's been so adamant about winning, there's no way he's not going to want to know whether he's been crowned."

"Yeah, maybe." I sniff, catching the roll of tissues Saylor chucks at me.

So dumb. I don't know why I'm getting all emotional over a guy I've known less than a week. But as I stare at his gingerbread house, *I know*. It's the same feeling I had a couple of nights ago on our date. It's because, to Alex, I was nothing more than Haven who owns the tree shop.

For the first time in four years, I was myself. He took me away from my worries about money, and how I was going to plan my future. What I was going to *do* with myself. Instead, I got to *be.*

You're a human being, not a human doing, my mom used to say. And this week is the first time I truly understand what she meant.

It also made me realize how much I crave human touch. And not just the fling of a passing tourist. I've been so bogged down in sorting my life out, I hadn't stopped to enjoy it. Alex has been the combination of fresh air and the hefty kick up the ass I needed. I've already decided that "making time for myself" is going at the top of my New Year's resolutions—ones I plan on keeping—and that includes dating.

Now I just need to figure out how I can find a six-foot-three Englishman with brilliant blue eyes who lives in Aspen, or at least within a twenty-mile radius.

"Dry your tears, Havey, we got visitors," announces Saylor.

I blow my nose, turning to find the visitors I've been waiting for all morning. All four of them, walking through the doors of the bakery.

"God*damn*. What are they putting in the water over there?" Saylor mutters under her breath, moving to stand next to me, because she's never seen the four of them together, and the first time is an *experience.*

It's clear they're set apart from anyone I've ever met; the only other time I'd seen them together was the night at the bar, but this morning, in daylight, there's an air of nobility and dignity surrounding them I hadn't noticed before.

All the same height, same long legs and broad chests, same arresting bright blue eyes, full mouths, and dark stubble. One of the twins has a baseball cap on with the Aspen Valley Polo Club logo—*Miles*. Which means it's Hendricks with his rich brown hair flopping in that deliberately mussed up way—perfectly imperfect. And they're both wearing identical mischievous grins, their dimples popping. I feel my cheeks glow, because I'm wondering if Alex has told them about what we did. What I did to him, what he did to me. Whether they can tell by simply looking.

I shake it off and glance at Lando. He's the darkest of the four, his hair is curlier, his stubble almost classifies as a beard, which kind of matches his brooding personality. Even if you didn't know he's the eldest, *you'd know*. There's a seriousness about him that's not present in the others.

Then there's the only one I have eyes for—Alex—his chocolatey brown waves flicked away from his smooth brow like he's just run his fingers through it. It's making me want to run *my fingers* through it.

"Hey." Alex grins.

"Hey."

"Hi, Haven." The twins chorus in sync, to which Lando rolls his eyes.

"Hi, guys."

"Came to collect my prize."

I shake my head at Alex, with a grin. "How do you know you've won?"

"I won," he replies, holding my gaze.

"The prizes are announced at three p.m."

"We'll be in the air, our flight leaves after lunch." Alex's bottom lip pouts in exaggeration, and he reaches out to take my hand. "You need to tell me."

"Oh, put him out of his misery," says Miles. "He'll be bloody unbearable the whole way home otherwise."

"Okay…" I point over to the display where the winners are laid out. "They're all there. Your house won Most Creative."

Hendricks and Miles whoop and rush

over to the table, triumph spreads across Alex's face as pulls me into him.

"I knew it," he murmurs, smacking his lips to mine.

"Pays to sleep with the judge," calls Miles from across the bakery as he inspects the rest of the entries, and behind me, Saylor barks out a laugh. "Ooh, this one's a good one."

"Hey, ours is a bloody good house. I didn't need to sleep with the judge to win it." Alex protests, and brings his lips closer to my ear. "But I couldn't stop myself."

My body goes from warmish to boiling hot in less than a second.

"It's quite the entertainment out there." Lando nods toward the band. It's getting busy; the food trucks are setting up, and now the music is quieter, more people are hanging around.

It's still terrible though.

I grimace. "Sorry about the Christmas music."

"Is that what it is?" replies Alex. "I like it."

"What?"

"I can't tell what they're playing. Doesn't sound anything like Christmas to me."

I crack a smile. "I guess that's a silver lining then."

"Sure is."

From the corner of my eye, I see Lando check his watch.

"Al, we need to be quick. Remember."

"Yeah yeah. Just pick what you want to take home and give me a minute." Alex waves him off, and Lando goes to hurry along the twins. "So…"

"So."

"I've had fun this week."

I stare up into his eyes and try to commit them to memory, but I already know I'd fail miserably. Pointless, anyway. "Me too. Thanks for helping at the bar, and buying all the gingerbread. And the decorations."

"You're welcome." He laughs, but it's kind of awkward.

This is kind of awkward, especially when Alex looks over to check on his brothers buying up everything that's coming out of the kitchen. There's a reason I hate goodbyes and it's this *awkwardness.* It almost ruins everything about the last few days, because it's clear neither of us knows what to say or what to do. I'm tempted to offer him my number, but again, what's the point? He lives seven thousand miles away. It's not like I can booty call him on the way home from The Old Saloon.

We're still standing there when Miles appears holding two large store bags. "Stocked up for the flight."

"Excellent."

"See you again, Haven. Thanks for keeping the Grinch occupied this week."

Alex shoots him a scowl, then turns to me. "I should go, but I wanted to come and say goodbye."

"Have a safe flight."

"Thank you." He leans in, his lips resting

against my cheek before he steps away.

The four of them file through the door, each of them turning to smile and wave one last time before they disappear out of sight.

And that's that. My Christmas fling has flung.

I get through the rest of the day on autopilot; serving customers, thanking the participants, announcing the winners, and presenting the check.

And in between, I try not to cry.

Merry Christmas

Alexander

16

"You know what? I'm not coming home with you. I'm going to stay another day. I'll see you Monday," I spit out before I have a chance to change my mind.

Lando pauses with his hand on the car door, a slow smile spreads across his face. "You want me to send the plane back for you?"

I shake my head. "No, there's a British Airways flight in the morning. Just ask James to have someone waiting at Heathrow to collect me, will you?"

"Sure." He slaps me on the back as

Miles throws a couple of bags in the trunk, carefully placing his snowboard on top. "You do what you need to do. But before I go, thanks for this week. I couldn't have made it through without you."

"We've had some fun, haven't we? You ready to get home and face the music?"

"Caroline and Jeremy?"

"Nope. Mum finding you a new wife." A laugh rips out of me.

Lando shakes his head. "I don't think so. We all know being single and staying single is in my future. I have no intention of getting into another relationship. I've learned my lesson."

"Can I be there when you tell her?"

"If you'd like. It's the least I can do after this week." Lando pulls me into a hug and kisses my cheek. "See you Monday. Maybe I'll collect you if you're lucky."

"One of your lowly subjects, Your Grace? I'm honored." I chuckle. "But I'll be expecting a welcome home banner in the arrivals hall."

"I'll see what I can do." He laughs, and giving me one last squeeze, gets into the car.

I wait while the rest of the skis, luggage, and the two life-sized nutcracker statues are loaded in the second car behind.

"You're really staying?" asks Hendricks, holding the bag of cinnamon buns we collected earlier, and I'm sorely tempted to ask him to leave me a couple. But I can get some later.

"I am. Tell Max his favorite uncle will see him on Monday."

"Bloody hell," he replies with a shake of his head and ducks into the car next to Lando.

I get the impression none of them are surprised by my announcement. Even more so when Miles ropes me into a bigger hug than Lando did.

"Proud of you, bro. And thanks for the dare you won me. I'll make sure it lands favorably on you next time we're playing snap."

"What?"

"Lando traded me his turn."

"You bet I'd stay?" I ask, confused.

"Sure did. I convinced the duke to wager his first go, seeing as he lost this week."

"You didn't do too badly out of it," shouts a voice from inside the car, but I'm still trying to wrap my head around this conversation.

"Hang on. I only decided this morning…"

"Nope. You decided that day in the tree shop." He pats my face, the ear-to-ear smile of his never faltering. "I know you too well, big brother. Not everyone's cut out for the casual sex life, it's okay. Nothing to be ashamed of."

"I'm not ashamed. What—"

"I'm just saying, it's okay to have feelings." He shrugs. "Me, I like to keep things simple. But you—"

"Miles, get in the car," Henricks interrupts before Miles finishes his sentence.

With a wink and an overly exaggerated salute, he does, sliding into the back seat next to Hendricks as the car engines start up.

I take a deep breath. I don't have feelings, not how he means. Like *feelings.* I'm staying because I don't need to be home until Monday. That's all. Oh, and because I need to say a better goodbye to Haven. I can't leave her with that poor excuse for one from earlier.

"See you boys in two days." I slam the door shut and tap on the roof.

It takes a few minutes before they leave—after Miles runs back inside because he decides he needs to pee—and I watch the cars drive off through the gates.

They're barely out of the driveway before I sprint for the shower.

An hour later, I'm standing outside the bakery for the second time today.

It's impressive how quickly they've managed to tidy the place up—the temporary stands have been removed, the terrible band isn't deafening everyone with unrecognizable Christmas music. The competition's over, and there aren't a thousand people standing outside waiting to find out who won. The street is relatively empty, save for a few shoppers wandering into other stores along the way.

Dusk is setting in, so it's easier to spot Haven and Saylor inside. I can see them through the window, laughing as they wipe down the counters. Haven's whole face lights up with a smile, and I know her boobs are jiggling under her apron. I'm tempted to watch for a little longer just so I can remember this moment, even the boob jiggling, but only because I like seeing her laugh.

Me, watching a girl laugh. I'm so glad Miles can't hear my thoughts.

I don't know what's happened to me this week. It's not just the sex—okay, maybe it's the sex—but there's no way that *just sex* would have had me missing a flight home. This isn't going to make her easier to forget. Quite the contrary. Yet here we are. Miles has already been correct too many times this week for my liking to be also correct about feelings. So, I push that thought away.

But obviously because Miles is Miles, my phone buzzes right at that second.

It's a photo of a box of condoms.

Miles: *Left a present on your bed. Wrap it up and enjoy, big brother. Love you. xx*

And with that I hurry toward the store as Saylor disappears into the kitchens.

"We're shut," Haven announces without looking around from the bottom shelf she's cleaning. "Open again at seven tomorrow."

"Thought you might want one more night with the crowning champion of the gingerbread houses."

Her hand stops wiping. Slowly, she turns and lifts her chin, and her green eyes meet mine.

"Wh-what are you doing here?"

I raise a shoulder. "Guess I wanted one more night too."

"You stayed in Aspen?"

I nod. "Looks like I did."

She peers around me, before her eyes find mine again. "On your own?"

"On my own." I grin. "So I'm going to need you to come and keep me company. Don't want to be rattling around the house by myself."

We both turn to the kitchen doors as they swing open, and Saylor walks through. She stops dead when she spots me, her brows knotting together. "Hey, it's the English muffin, thought you'd left."

"I didn't."

"I see that."

I glance back at Haven. "What d'you say? Want to keep me company?"

Her teeth sink into her bottom lip as she thinks about it. It's all show though. I can see from the way her pupils dilated the second they landed on me that one way or another, we're spending the night together.

"Um, Say…d'you mind if I take off."

Saylor grins wide. "Hey, I've been praying all week you'd ask."

"You don't pray."

"For you I do, now scram." She shoos her hands at Haven and turns to me. "Make sure she can't walk in the morning."

"Jes*us*, Saylor," Haven splutters, her cheeks turning that shade of pink I've become obsessed with.

"I'll do my best. It's not like I haven't been trying."

"Oh God loves a trier, honey," she shoots back, and Haven tugs me through the door toward the car, to the sound of Saylor laughing her arse off.

"Holy shit, this view. There's a pool…"

I'm already stripping off. "Time is of the essence. Sit on my face, then I'll fuck you in there while you're watching the sunset. It's heated, don't worry."

"The sun's set already. It's dark."

"Oh, well, sunrise then," I reply, stepping out of my boxers. "Why am I the only one naked?"

Haven turns around, her mouth dropping open.

"Alex!"

"Yes?"

Her hand sweeps toward the wall of windows. "Someone will see."

"Sweetheart, no one's seeing anything. It's totally private out there." I find the dimmer switch and turn the mood lighting down until we're only lit by the glow of the fire and a few strategically placed lamps. But the expression on her face tells me she's not quite sure. "I promise."

I, for one, don't really mind a little voyeurism—

you grow up in the countryside, and at some point someone's going to walk past you while you're balls deep in your girlfriend, banging her against the barn door.

But Haven…no, not Haven. I don't want to share her with anyone. She's mine. No one gets to see her how I see her.

I take a step toward her, my dick thickening with each stride. Her breath shallows as she watches, her eyes darting between the window and me.

"Haven…do you honestly think I'd allow anyone to see you naked except me?" I don't know why I'm talking about her like this thing with us will continue after tonight, like there's a future to my words. But I can't help myself. Right now, in this moment, I mean everything I say.

"Um—"

I stop in front of her. Using the tip of my finger I brush away the thick strands of hair almost covering her face, then tilt her chin so she's looking at me. I want her to see how serious I am.

"Do you think I'd allow anyone a single glimpse of your perfect body?"

My hands push up under her sweater; her belly quivers from that first touch of my skin on hers. It shoots across my body like lightning.

"No one gets to see you like I do. No one sees these incredible tits…"

She groans as I remove her bra, tossing it to the floor to join the sweater, and sucks in her plump lower lip as my thumb swipes over her hardened nipple. I'm not lying. Haven has the most incredible tits I've ever seen; heavy, pert, and fitting perfectly into my hand. I could spend hours on them and never get bored.

"I'm going to miss these." I kiss one then the other, while ghosting my hands down the curve of her waist and into her jeans, where I pop the button. But these aren't the jeans she was wearing the other night. The other night they had a zip and these are all buttons…and they don't want to fucking pop.

I'm so desperate to taste her, feel her come apart as my tongue slides inside her for one last night, that I'm clumsily tugging them off. Too clumsy, clearly, when she starts laughing.

"You want me to do it?"

"Please." I grin, crossing my arms as she kindly obliges.

And when they hit the floor, I gesture to the underwear she's left on and need to be removed. White cotton knickers with a candy cane right at the apex of her thighs. Seeing them makes my dick so impossibly hard, I'm tempted to steal them to take home with me. But for now, I'll settle on them joining the rest of her clothes on the floor.

And then she's as gloriously naked as I am.

I lean in and my dick juts against her stomach. "You know, if I fuck you well enough, we could steam all the windows up. Then we'll definitely be private."

Her squeal of laughter bounces off the hard surfaces as I toss her over my shoulder, giving her ass a quick slap, and pull her onto the couch until she's exactly where I want her to be. Sitting on my face.

"Ohh…" is all she can manage as my tongue spears through her soaked slit as she jostles around to find her balance, and I get to work.

The scent of her is so fucking addictive.

I'm treated to the most perfect sight. Haven arched back, holding her tits and tugging on her nipples, while her thighs are clamped around my head. The best vise.

She may as well be my last meal, because after tonight, I'm gone…so I'm feasting like she is. Spread out on my face, her arousal drips down my chin.

"Ahhh, Alex," she moans when my thumb circles her clit, adding pressure with each swipe. "Oh fu-fuck. How…I'm…coming. Ohhhh."

Her first orgasm rips through her, thighs squeezing my face as she grinds down on me. I don't stop, I don't let up. I want her begging for mercy. The speed at which she comes has me so hard it's almost painful, and she's still coming when I wrap my arms around her waist, lift her as I sit up, and drag her onto her knees.

There's a split second between lining myself up with her and pushing inside her with a cry.

I don't even think about it. Not once does it occur to me that I've not sheathed up.

The sensation of being bare is so incredible I stop moving. *Then* I realize.

"Oh fuck. Haven…"

"Wh-why'd you stop?"

I pull back, not all the way but most of it. I can't quite bring myself to leave this snug, cozy warmth. And the sight of her round, juicy arse is too good. "I need to go and get condoms, they're upstairs." *Thank you, Miles.*

"I'm on the pill."

I pause, *again.* "Really?"

"Yeah."

"Because"—I slide back inside her half an inch—"we should be careful."

Haven pushes back onto me another inch and clenches. "We should. I agree."

"But you're on the pill."

"I am."

"And I can pull out."

Another clench. "Sure, do that. Good idea."

My conscience is stretched paper thin. It would literally take a second to run upstairs and grab the box on my bed, and all I need to do is think about what happened to Hendricks. But on the other hand…I'm inside Haven, and her pussy is the best thing I've ever experienced in my life. Absolutely *unreal.*

Warm, tight, wet. Just for me.

Because I'm taking too long to make a decision, she takes it out of my hand and pushes right back onto me. "Fuck me, Alex."

So I do.

Fisting her hair in my hand, I yank her back. Her mouth collides with mine as I drive into her, and I swallow every single one of her cries. It's rough and desperate. This is the goodbye we deserve. Not some fucking weird moment in a bakery surrounded by an audience where I kiss her cheek.

I want her to feel me in every inch of her body until we meet again. And I'm going to spend all night making sure of it. I need to because I'm not going to last this first time around.

My balls are rock hard, there's a pressure twisting my spine with an intensity I've never felt before.

"Al…ex. Fu-u-ck." She cries out as I slap her arse.

Her thighs clamp, and I know she's close. I ease the grip on her hair and grab onto her arse, holding her still while I give her everything I have. Plunging into her over and over, harder and deeper. I don't stop until I feel that first vicious clench of her pussy, which is enough to send me over the edge.

I pull out right before I explode, tugging my cock and finish all over her. It's everywhere. Her hair, her back, dripping down between her cheeks. She's painted in my come. If I wasn't already on my knees, the view of her like this would have brought me to them.

It's spectacular. *She's* spectacular.

I catch sight of the clock. There are twelve hours until I have to leave, and I intend to make the most of every single second.

We stop to shower and eat. Haven cooks, while I watch her and wonder how the hell I met her. We steam the windows up. We fuck everywhere, only this time using the present Miles left for me. It's not until sometime around four a.m. that we collapse exhausted on the giant couch and I chase her into sleep.

The sunrise wakes me, turning the mountains orange, and it takes a second for me to blink away the brightness. Gently, I remove the strands of Haven's damp hair stuck in my beard and brush it back while trying to remember a time when I felt more content.

I can't.

Leaving it as long as I can before easing out of the blanket carefully, I make sure I do so with minimal disturbance. I needn't have worried, Haven is out for the count, and I jog up the stairs to the shower feeling all kinds of smug. I won't forget this in a hurry. I won't forget her, *ever*. It's laughable I thought I even could.

I've fucked her into a coma.

I'm surprised my dick hasn't fallen off this week from the amount of sex we've had, and I bet it'll be a long time before she meets someone who makes her come like I did.

I stop dead in my stride, almost winded by the jealousy punching me in the gut at that thought. When I leave, Haven will meet someone else. It's inevitable, of course she will. She's an insanely amazing woman.

Except…the thought of her meeting

someone else *infuriates* me.

She'll have sex with the next dickhead who picks her up at the jukebox. Or who buys a lifetime supply of cinnamon buns. And that *won't do.* I don't want some fumbling cowboy sloppily humping her to completion, when she should be treated like a goddess and worshipped for the rest of time.

No one should get to witness her falling apart like I did.

Even though I'm seven thousand miles away and have an entire life back in England, I'm thinking about how I can reasonably stop Haven being with any other guy.

I think about it through my shower, the final bits of packing, and taking the remainder of my shit downstairs to leave by the front door, and I'm no closer to an answer because *I can't* stop her.

This was a fling and nothing more. We both know it.

I pull on my boxers and creep back under the blanket, fitting into Haven's curled body so well she barely stirs.

"I need to leave soon," I whisper, moving her hair to the side so I can run my lips along her shoulder. "But you can stay as long as you want. Take a shower, get in the hot tub. The car will come back for you to take you home when you're ready."

"Hmm," she breathes out, stretching from her sleep and looping her arm back to wrap around my neck. "Thank you."

"You're welcome."

When she stays quiet, I close my eyes again. Breathing her in, trying to commit the last week of her to memory. I need to take a piece of her back home with me.

"That's the tree I sold you," she murmurs.

I nod. Only the twinkly lights are left on it after Miles removed all the decorations to take home, including the star on top. It's bare, but also kind of beautiful in its simplicity.

Haven's staring at it, while I'm treated to the sight of her naked back, tracing my fingers down the ridges of her spine. The clock says I have about twenty minutes before the car comes to take me to the airport. I *know* I could do a lot with Haven in twenty minutes.

"My dad died at Christmas," I find myself saying. "He was going to pick out a tree for me and a car crashed into him. He died instantly."

Haven stops running her fingers up and down my bicep. After a minute she twists in my arms so we're face to face. I can't escape the look she has. The sorrow. "How long ago was this?"

"Twenty years ago, tomorrow," I reply quietly, my eyes dropping away.

"Alex…you were a little boy."

"I know." I swallow thickly. "He would be here if it weren't for me. It's why I hate Christmas. But this year, meeting you, has made me hate it a little bit less, and I wanted you to know that."

Her hands push through my hair, she twists the ends around her fingers. It's gentle and soothing and I don't want it to stop.

"Both my parents died from cancer. My mom

went first, and had huge medical bills. I didn't find out until after my dad died that he'd been struggling to pay them. The reason I've been working so much is because I need to pay off all the debts he left so I don't lose the business, or the home I've known since I was born."

My eyes shoot open. I want to say something, but I don't know what. I have more money than I know what to do with. More than I'll ever know what to do with. There's nothing I can say that would make her think I understand what it's like to have that struggle. I only know what it's like to lose a parent.

Haven stops me regardless. "I'm telling you this because shit things happen, and there's nothing we can do. It's not our fault, and you can't blame yourself for your dad dying any more than it helps for me to be pissed at my parents for leaving me in this mess for the past few years. I usually miss my parents the most at Christmas. It's hard and painful, especially when I'm so busy I can barely think, because then I feel guilty." She smiles at me. "But this year, meeting you, gave me a little bit of the fun I'd been missing. I've been needing."

I lie there, my mind full of thoughts about how similar we are.

Two people on the other sides of the world brought together through a love (her) hate (me) relationship with Christmas. I know I have to go home, but it's not stopping me from trying to find reasons to come back.

My eyes fall on one of the practice gingerbread houses sitting on the far table.

"You know, I *am* going to have to come back and defend my crown as most creative."

She lifts an eyebrow. "Oh?"

"Yeah. I can't let the Rivern family swoop back in and take it, can I?"

Haven shakes her head, her beautiful honey-gold hair, all tussled up from a night of my fingers running through it, sweeps over her shoulders. "I guess not."

"So…what do you say? Same time next year?"

She chews on the end of her thumb, prolonging my misery of whether she'll agree to this ridiculous idea. I mean, who's to say we'll even be single in a year. Though, *again*, the thought of her with someone else has my teeth gritting and fists clenching.

My phone buzzes with a message telling me the car service is two minutes away. I ease up off the couch, spy the clothes I'd laid out for traveling home, and tug on my jeans. I'm almost completely dressed, and she's still not said anything.

"I can do same time next year." She peers up, batting her thick lashes at me, with a grin I'd kiss off her if I didn't have to make this stupid flight.

"Yes?"

"Yes."

"So, it's settled then." The couch dips as I sit down and pull on my sneakers.

"Hey, what's your last name?"

"My last name?"

She nods. The gate bell buzzes.

"Yeah, I don't know it."

"Oh." I pause. "It's Burlington. Alex Burlington."

"See you next year, Alex Burlington."

I drop a kiss on her swollen, pink lips. "See you next year, Haven Wylder."

To be continued...

Merry Christmas

Epilogue

Valentine Nook —
a village in the Cotswolds, Oxfordshire

LANDO

Six months later

There's nowhere more beautiful than the English countryside.

It's what Shakespeare, Wordsworth, Blake, and their contemporaries wrote about for reams on end. They managed to perfectly capture the essence of what it's like to be among the rolling green hills, surrounded by horses gently grazing in the fields, a brook babbling somewhere in the distance, the familiar twitter of birds in their nests…

Their words are tangible, and every time I arrive back from London, I can almost feel them welcoming me home. It's the perfect antidote to a few days spent in the city. I usually only need to take a deep breath of country air, saddle up my horse, Thunder, and the tension in my shoulders melts away to nothing.

Not today.

It all started an hour ago as I was driving under the old stone arch—the words *amor principum* carved into its center. It marks the threshold to the village of Valentine Nook, one of the oldest villages in Oxfordshire, the heart of the countryside, and has belonged to my family for five hundred years.

Often described as the most beautiful and romantic place in England, it's believed that Valentine Nook is where you will meet your true love, and according to legend, it's where Cupid was conceived—hence its name. Cupid's parents—the gods Venus and Mars came down from Mount Olympus for a tryst near an ancient glen on the outskirts of the village. Nine happy months later, Cupid made his entrance, and the concept of love has never been the same.

Just like my family, the people who live in Valentine Nook have been here for generations too.

There's Leon & Daughters, the local butcher

who used to be Leon & Sons when his grandfather owned the place, but after he married and had four girls, his eldest daughter made him change the name. Next door is the bakery, where the best sourdough east of San Francisco is made, and people come from miles around to grab the early loaves on a Saturday morning, along with a coffee from the shop across the road.

Two pubs, The Cupid's Arrow and The One True Love, both alike in…just kidding, this isn't Romeo and Juliet, they don't hate each other. But they do stand at opposite ends of Valentine High Street, in constant, *albeit friendly*, competition, usually over who has the biggest blooms on their hanging baskets (Cupid's Arrow), who makes the best pork pie (The One True Love), and who will win the annual Valentine Nook cricket match (currently 34–29 to The Cupid's Arrow.) On the opposite side is the vets, where you'll find my brother Hendricks when he's not out helping to birth the new season's cows or locating a runaway goat for Mrs. Winston.

There's a church with the vicar who's always running late because he misplaced his glasses, a fishmonger, a beauty salon, and the village store—The Valentine Cook, which stocks everything you could possibly need, plus anything you didn't realize you needed.

At the other end of the high street to the stone arch stands the fountain.

Modeled off the Trevi Fountain in Rome but on a much smaller scale, ours has Cupid sitting atop, instead of Oceanus, where he aims his arrow at any unsuspecting passersby. Just like the Trevi, year-round visitors come to throw in coins and make a wish they'll finally meet their soul mate.

All the money collected from the fountain goes toward paying for the upkeep of the village—keeping the rose bushes and flower beds tidy, the cricket pitch in good shape, and the hedgerows trimmed. The lampposts, fences, and buildings all receive a regular lick of fresh paint. It finances the Summer Fair, which is next week, the Christmas Fair in December, and the Halloween party for all the local children. It won't come as any surprise to hear the majority of funds go toward Valentine's Day. Because Valentine's Day in Valentine Nook is…well, I'm sure you can imagine.

I don't think you'd find a more perfect village.

It's my favorite place in the world.

Unfortunately, every village has its idiot…or

something along those lines.

Ours is *Agatha Chase*. A self-appointed high witch, specializing in the services of love, and just like everyone else here, her family goes back generations.

She owns Agatha Chase's Love Emporium, where she brews potions and spells that she believes will summon your soul mate. She gives readings, she hosts full moon parties, and the twins swear they see her dancing naked in her garden at least twice a month.

If I didn't think the villagers would riot, I'd have evicted her years ago. But annoyingly, Agatha's good for the local economy.

The people who are throwing coins in the fountain, which fund the village's upkeep, are mostly here because they're visiting Agatha. Once they're done, they drink at the pub, or grab lunch from Mary's Sandwich Shop, and buy a tea towel or tote bag from the village store that says they came to Cupid's birthplace. Sometimes, if they're lucky enough to get a room, there's a delightful bed-and-breakfast run by Mr. and Mrs. Kilpatrick, though it's always booked up six months in advance.

I forgot to mention Valentine Nook is the number one place to propose marriage.

But mostly, people come for Agatha.

When my father was alive, he used to think she added a bit of fun. I *don't* share his opinion. In fact, I try my best to avoid her at all costs.

Why? Because Agatha Chase has declared that I will be alone forever.

(Cue, eye roll.)

It first started a decade ago when I accidentally bumped into her while I was coming out of The One True Love. She brushed past me, grabbed my hand with a screech, and promptly professed she'd had a premonition. I'm not going to lie, I panicked a little. The next morning when I'd sobered up and thought about it logically, I decided it was all bollocks. I'd been twenty-three and had no intention of settling down any time soon.

Over the years it became somewhat of a running joke in my family and close friendship circle especially, as one of "England's most eligible bachelors," I was never short of women interested in me. There's no way I'd end up alone. Every so often I would take them on a date in the village, just to prove to Agatha Chase that she had it all wrong.

And then I met Caroline Montague.

It was the day I turned thirty-one. I'd been celebrating in London with a group of my friends, when I saw her across the crowded bar. The attraction had been immediate—a classic English rose with flawless creamy skin and glossy dark hair, I couldn't stop staring at her—and after a couple of dates I decided she was The One. My mother had already started up her campaign to find the next Duchess of Oxfordshire, and on paper, Caroline had been the perfect girl.

For reasons I could never figure out, no one really seemed to like Caroline. But I chose not to question why, pushed it to the back of my head, and ignored it all. It didn't matter that we didn't laugh together much or we had little in common, who needs those things when you're in love?

And we lived in the most romantic village in England. What more could we want?

Over the last six months, I've realized the tiny niggles that constantly followed me around were, in fact, giant red flags waving in my face. Ones I refused to acknowledge until the evening before our wedding when I walked in on Caroline fucking my ex–best friend.

Losing a friend and a fiancée in one night was hard enough to deal with, but since then two further issues have arisen.

One, Agatha Chase has taken to reminding me of her premonition every chance she gets. Even if she's correct, I don't want to hear it. Therefore, I cut her off the second she opens her mouth.

The second, slightly more exasperating matter, is my mother, who, since my engagement ended, has attempted to set me up with *every single woman* in British high society.

I've declined them all, because I have no intention of dating again any time soon.

Ironic that the grumpy, cynical man doomed to be single forever is the owner of the most romantic village in England, isn't it?

Anyway, as I was saying…my drive through the village this morning—and subsequently my good mood—was totally ruined.

It began as I passed the fountain and spied a larger than usual number of visitors crowded around it. Not that I count, but I don't normally have to wait for them to move out of the way, and was too deep in thought about what could have caused it to notice the giant moving vans parked outside Bluebell Cottage, where I used to live with Caroline.

I haven't stepped inside since I found her and Jeremy against the entrance wall.

Slamming the brakes, I make a sharp turn to avoid hitting a pile of boxes in the middle of the road and stop the car.

Not the *best* place to leave a pile of boxes, I feel. And then I realize there are boxes everywhere. Boxes from the three giant vans, taking up almost the entire width of the road.

Peering into the open end of the nearest van, I spy several large house plants, furniture covered in movers' blankets, framed prints…nothing that looks like decorating equipment—the only explanation I'd accept. But I already know it's not that. The sixth sense twitching in my gut provides an unnecessary warning. The cottage was redecorated a few months ago, and since then, it's been empty.

Bluebell Cottage is something I've filed away under the subject of *Things I Don't Want to Deal With Right Now,* which you'll also find next to

Love Life.

"Watch it, mate," yells one of the movers, shaking me from my darkening mood.

I lower my window, prop an elbow on the door frame, and lean out. "Could you explain to me what's going on here?"

Another couple of movers carrying a large, Bubble-Wrapped, and heavy—from the way their knees are tensed—object, stop and stare at me. Because *obviously* they're moving furniture. Moving furniture into *my* house.

"Whatsit look like we're doin'?"

I point to Bluebell's front door. "It looks like you're moving furniture into that cottage."

"Proper Einstein right here, fellas." The mover laughs and continues on his way.

In the rearview mirror, I watch the rest of them shaking their head in amusement as I shift into reverse, maneuver past the boxes, and hit the gas, taking off for Burlington Hall, my home.

I might not have the full picture of what's happening, but *I know* that somehow my mother has everything to do with it.

Normally when I approach Burlington, I like to slow the car and take my time driving through the gates. I love the way the road sweeps past the fields—currently slightly parched from the summer sun—and the horses grazing, high above the valley where the stables and polo ground lies.

If Thunder is out, he gallops over to run alongside, whinnying for a scratch and any possible carrots or Polo mints I might have with me, and I'll stop to oblige him for five minutes.

Farther along, the herd of Aberdeen Angus dot the horizon, and it's here where the turrets of Burlington Hall appear in the distance, growing larger and larger as the car continues its journey. It's only when you turn the corner and pass through the long line of oak trees standing proudly like sentinels, that it fully comes into view.

A vast structure of pale Cotswold stone, set in three sides of a square with neat rows of arched windows across two floors, the asymmetrical turrets breaking up the chimneys staggered across the roof make it look ever-so-slightly French.

It's magnificent.

And my breath catches the first time I see it.

Every time. I'm filled with pride and gratitude for this place that's housed my family for five hundred years.

Now, however, I'm too annoyed to take it in. I don't even get to enjoy what a perfect June day it is, the sun high in a cloudless kingfisher-blue sky. Instead, screeching to a halt outside the front doors, I sprint out and go in search of answers.

"Mother?" My holler echoes off the hard surfaces of the entrance hall and the wide pillars on either side of the vestibule. "Mum, where are you?"

I stand there and wait, but there's no answer. The only sound I hear is the barking of dogs getting louder, their nails clattering on the stone floor as they rush down the hallway to greet me. It's possible my mum's choosing to ignore me. Her pet peeve with us as kids was when we stood and yelled for someone, instead of going to find them. Our argument being, it was far quicker than spending half an hour searching around while they could be moving from room to room.

But today, I have no intention of waiting, and one way or another I'm getting answers.

I'm only slowed down on my mission when

three of the labradors—Hamish, Maud, and Dolly—catch up with me, because they all demand I say hello to them before they follow me through the house and back outside.

"Mother!" I try again, marching over the newly mowed grass toward my first stop, the pool, which the dogs immediately launch themselves into.

Giant floats—a unicorn, a fire engine, and a dragon—bob in the center; Max, my three-year-old nephew, has clearly been here, except the only person I find is my sister, Clementine, lying on a navy and white striped sun lounger with her nose deep in a book. Eleven years younger than me, she's just taken her finals, and since she arrived back home a couple of weeks ago, she's been permanently installed by the pool.

"Where's Mum?"

Clementine tilts her head toward me and slowly pulls down the nose of her sunglasses until she's peering at me through her Burlington-blue eyes, the ones we all inherited from our late father.

"Oh, hey, Lanny, when did you get here?"

"Thirty seconds ago, d'you know where Mum

is?"

She shrugs, totally lacking interest in whatever has me agitated, and returns to her book. "Dunno, she might be in the kitchens, or I think she talked about going over to the vegetable gardens. Or it might be the rose garden. I can't remember."

I grunt to myself. Typical. Turning to leave, I then spin back around and narrow my eyes at my sister.

Clementine normally has her ear to the ground with anything happening around here, especially when it concerns things that *shouldn't* be happening. If anyone knows what's going on in the village, she will.

"You don't know what's happening at Bluebell Cottage, do you? There are moving vans blocking the lane."

Clementine abruptly sits up and shifts onto her knees, which I should take as my first warning. This time she whips off her sunglasses, and her expression—only moments ago somewhat blasé and disinterested—is wide with excitement.

Too much excitement for my liking. Especially when she gasps and claps her hands in rapid fire.

"Holy shit. *Today*? You saw them, *today*? She's

here already. Oh my god!"

"What?" My brows draw together in confusion. "I asked you about moving vans."

"Yes!" her screech almost bursts my eardrum. "You really saw them? They were definitely outside Bluebell?"

"Saw what? Clementine, why are there moving vans outside the cottage?"

"Mum's put a new tenant in. You'll never guess who it is—"

"What?!" I explode.

"The new tenant, guess who she is? *Guess*, Lanny!" She balls her hands, pumping them in the air. "Oh my god, let's go down and meet her now. We can take her a housewarming gift."

My fists clench, my blood boils, my molars are on the verge of breaking from how hard I'm clenching them. This time my mother has gone too far, and from the look on Clementine's face, she seems to have roped my sister in too.

"She? *She?*" I snap. "Un-fucking-believable."

"Wait for me!" cries Clementine, totally misreading the way I storm off. "I just need to change. Go and grab a bottle of champagne from the fridge."

I most certainly am *not* getting champagne.

I march back over the lawns and into the house, the way I came. Storming down the corridor, I briefly peer into each room I pass—my study, the library, Max's playroom—but my mother is nowhere in sight. I'm about to take the stairs two at a time when I sense a movement next to me, and I know instinctively it's James Winters, our family director of operations. The *ninja*.

In hindsight, he should have been my first stop, seeing as anything my mother is involved with includes him too.

"Your Grace, if I may—"

My fist tightens around the banister. "Oh, for fuck's sake, James, there's no one else around. You practically raised me, drop the officiality, will you?"

He tuts loudly; he knows exactly why I'm boiling with rage, and it dawns on me that my mother's absence is purposeful. James is waiting for me as the voice of reason, because after our father died, that was the role he took. The five of us children were nothing compared to the thousands of troops he commanded as a former army brigadier.

"I was going to say you can't do anything about it."

"Like hell I can't." I sprint up the stairs, only for James to follow.

"Lando, I know you're pissed off, but you can't kick her out. She signed the lease, and she's here until the end of the year."

She. *Her.* It's the only part of James's sentence that has my jaw clenching.

"I didn't okay it. This is *my* land, it's *my* cottage. *I* am the duke. *I* am in charge. *Not* my mother."

James sighs but says nothing more. I know he agrees with me, but I also know he'll do anything my mother asks of him.

"I know exactly what's going on here," I snap. "And don't pretend like you don't either. I thought at the very least you'd have had my back in this dating agency she seems to be running."

"Of course, I have your back, Lando. But you haven't exactly been *you* the last six months. Ever since…" his voice tails off.

"Ever since I walked in on Caroline fucking Jeremy?" I snap.

"Yes."

"And how exactly do you want me to be?"

"Well—" He waves at my face—more precisely, the beard, which has grown thick and fast since I returned from Aspen.

"Yes?"

"You look like a yeti, for one. When was the last time you shaved?"

I scratch through the thick bush. I haven't been clean shaven since my wedding day, and beyond a couple of necessary trims, I haven't touched it. What's more, I like it.

"Six months ago. Caroline hated me with a beard, so I'm bloody well keeping it like this."

James remains silent, only raising an eyebrow.

"What's the second?"

"Your short temper." He replies without hesitation. "It's not like you, Lando. I know what happened was shit—"

"That's not the problem," I interrupt, and carry on up the stairs, because I do not want to get into another conversation about Caroline.

When there's no response to my statement, I turn around and find James still where he was.

"What?"

"Then what?"

I sit down with a heavy sigh of defeat, twisting the gold signet ring on my pinkie. "I have a business to run here, a huge multi-billion pound business. We do good, important work. But all anyone seems to care about—and by anyone, I mean mum—is finding me a wife. I don't know who's worse, her or Agatha Chase. Can't you get her to focus on Milo? He's going to be much harder to get settled down," I add with a grumble.

James chuckles and joins me on the step. A wet Hamish waddles up the stairs and drops down on the one below us, dripping everywhere.

"So…are you going to tell me who I've rented Bluebell Cottage to, or do I have to guess? And why's Clemmie acting like it's Christmas morning?"

James reaches out and strokes Hamish's ears. "I don't know much about her. Her representatives managed it."

"Representatives? What does that mean?"

"It was her agent, I believe." He's waving his hands about while he tries to find the correct wording. "Perhaps a manager? I'm not sure which is which. Gerard, from the estate team, brought her credentials over and the duchess approved it."

"An agent? What sort of agent?"

"I'd need to check her name, but she's an actress. Quite well known, I believe."

"An *actress*?"

"Yes. American."

"An *American*? Has my mother run out of women in England?" I scoff, although the entire scenario is sounding more ridiculous by the second. Hamish groans loudly in agreement.

James shrugs. "Possibly. She's from Hollywood apparently, according to your sister. Won awards."

I turn to him, his face is still wearing the same impassive expression it always does. But usually his left eye twitches ever so slightly when he's joking, only not this time.

It has to be though.

"Are you joking? Is this a joke?"

"No. It's not a joke."

"You're telling me my mother has moved an actress into Bluebell Cottage. She's trying to set me up with an actress?"

"I'm not sure that's—"

"That's *exactly* what's happening here. Stop being so diplomatic. She can't hear you." I laugh, and suddenly, like the sun breaking through dark rainclouds, my mood lifts and a smile beams from my face.

My mother has truly outdone herself this time.

"An *American Hollywood actress*?" The laugh rumbles up my throat from deep in my belly, followed by another, until I'm laughing so hard I roll back on the stair. "An actress? Dear god. Really, James, you should have led with that. More fool my mother, I say."

"Lando…"

"There's no way I'd ever date an actress. Come on, let's saddle up the horses and ride over to the pub."

The Burlington boys will return in The Valentine Nook Chronicles - a brand new series coming in September 2025.

Valentine Nook is the first book in The Valentine Nook Chronicles, featuring Lando and his Hollywood superstar

(can you guess who she is?)

ACKNOWLEDGMENTS

If you're reading this in November / December, Happy Holidays.

There's something so magical about Christmas, even writing this in the dead of summer has made me want to drink cocoa, eat gingerbread and stand under the air-con wearing my favorite bobble hat and thick scarf.

This Christmas, this book, is a present to myself as well as to you lovely readers, because it's the start of a brand new series I literally can't stop thinking about. The fact that I already have a full series planned out is nothing short of a miracle, and one that's down to you all. I say it over and over but I wouldn't be here without you. I wouldn't be able to make up stories and live in fantasy land on a daily basis without your support. THANK YOU.

To Sam, who designed the most beautiful cover. I said I wanted a gingerbread house and boy did she deliver. I'm already chomping at the bit for the rest of the Valentine Nook Chronicles covers. I know she'll make them just as beautiful.

To Georgana, for your constant support of me and endlessly listening, helping me formulate ideas and giving me the best feedback. I'm so grateful.

To Valentine and everyone at Valentine PR, Taylor, Glav and Sydney. I'm so lucky to be working with you and all the help you give me in building the Luluverse. It's absolutely a team effort, and I couldn't do it without you.

Finally, to Logan, thank you being the first to listen to the audio. I so appreciate the time you took in helping it to be the best it could. You're an audio queen, and I bow to you.

For everyone else who makes the Luluverse turn, my world an easier place and the days just that little bit brighter. I adore you all.

Happy holidays, see you next year.

Lulu xo

ALSO BY LULU MOORE

The New York Players

Jasper

Cooper

Drew: The Vegas Edition (extended prologue)

Drew

Felix

Huck

The Tuesday Club

The Secret

The Suit

The Show

The New York Lions

The Third Baseman

The Shake Off

The Baller

The Strike Zone (coming April 2025)

Home Run (coming June 2025)

The Oxbridge Series

Oar With Friends

You Float My Boat - coming February 6 2025

The Valentine Nook Chronicles - coming September 2025

Once Upon A Christmas Tree

Valentine Nook

Wylder Ranch

Honeysuckle Lane

Foxleigh Park

Burlington Hall

ABOUT THE AUTHOR

Lulu started writing by accident, and somehow found herself stuck in a fictional world of ice hockey, baseball and billionaires. A world she has no plans to leave.

More recently she's ventured across the Atlantic to where her latest novel is set - the beautiful cities of Oxford and Cambridge, and the annual rowing showdown on the River Thames.

She's a big fan of strong heroines, because those fierce alphas need someone to keep them in check. You'll find her navigating her way through Romance Land one HEA at a time, and trying to figure out the latest social media platform she needs to post to.

She'd love to hear from you, loves hearing your opinions and thoughts, so please message her on any of the social platforms @lulumoorebooks and she'd love you to come and join her reader group on Facebook - aptly named The Jupiter Reeves Fan Club.

But if you don't want to do any of that, there's always her website - lulumoorebooks.com

Printed in Dunstable, United Kingdom

73490081R00211